"I have decided to marry you." Lord Alexander said it suddenly, without preamble, in a voice dripping with arrogant condescension.

The world whirled about her. She feared that for the first time in her life she might faint. Yet she collected herself and said tartly, "Now I imagine you are going to swear to me that you never gave the slightest thought to my sizable fortune?"

"I am not going to lie to you, Diana, but—"

"My name, my Lord Duke, is Miss Landale," she interrupted, her temper flaring. "And *I* have decided *not* to marry you!"

THE RELUCTANT HEIRESS

Marlene Suson

FAWCETT CREST • NEW YORK

A Fawcett Crest Book
Published by Ballantine Books
Copyright 1985 by Marlene Suson

Library of Congress Catalog Card Number: 84-91795

ISBN 0-449-20791-9

Manufactured in the United States of America

First Edition: May 1985

CHAPTER I

His Grace, the duke of Stratford, had decided to take a wife.

Since His Grace was both notorious for his many scandalous love affairs and hotly pursued as the nonpareil catch on the marriage market, this news would have excited intense curiosity among scores of eager mamas in whose minds the elusive duke's shocking morals were far outweighed by the desire to make a nubile daughter a duchess. Behind embroidered silk fans waving with agitation, the disappointed mamas would have asked who in the world was Alexander at last going to marry?

It was a question even the duke himself could not answer.

A scant half hour after His Grace had reached his decision to marry, his younger brother, Lord Charles Hadleigh, chanced to call upon him. His lordship found the duke in his private apartments, standing behind his Louis XV writing table and staring bleakly out a window at the leaden London sky.

Lord Charles had come in urgent need of yet another loan from Alexander to cover more unfortunate gambling losses, but his lordship was so startled by the somber look on the duke's face that he quite forgot the purpose of his visit.

"Whatever is the matter?" Lord Charles demanded, depositing himself on the moiré cushions of a French divan. "You look as though the devil himself has paid you a visit."

"Perhaps he has, Charlie," the duke responded grimly, and sank back into silence.

Never had Charlie seen his brother in such a black mood. His lordship's unease was heightened by the disarray cluttering the top of his elegant writing table, inlaid with satinwood marquetry. Why were account books and papers strewn across the table when the duke so prized order and neatness?

Alexander's gray eyes, which never failed to fix their observers with their penetrating stare, looked tired, as though he had slept little. He was nonetheless his usual picture of elegance in a double-breasted dressing gown of fawn-colored brocade. His hair, as black as the jet ring that he wore on his little finger, curled thickly about his handsome face. A fine straight nose flared slightly at the nostrils. His upper lip was a trifle thin, while the lower was full and slightly protruding.

The duke's reputation for arrogance was greatly enhanced by his right eyebrow. Unlike the left, which was a horizontal black slash, the right was sharply arched, like a haughty question mark.

Charlie pulled from his pocket an oval snuffbox of gold-and-green enamel that had been his late father's. "Don't keep me in suspense," he persisted. "What has happened?"

"I am getting married," Alexander said abruptly, looking as though he had just announced his imminent execution.

The snuffbox fell from Charlie's fingers and clattered to the floor. He could not have been more shocked if the duke had announced that he was forsaking the world for a monastery. "I say, are you serious? To whom? Surely not to—" Charlie managed to stop his wayward tongue before he named Lady Angela Bradwell, Alexander's current favorite.

"Not to Angela," His Grace said firmly.

Charlie struggled to hide his relief. Angela might be her-
alded by some as the most beautiful woman in London, but
she was one of the very few people that he did not like. Nor
was he surprised that his brother did not plan to marry her. It
would never do to introduce such a spoiled apple as Angela
into the Hadleigh family tree. The duke's bored, devil-may-
care facade might fool the world, but Charlie knew how seriously his brother took his duties and responsibilities as
head of the illustrious House of Hadleigh. He might enjoy
his flings with the likes of Lady Bradwell, but his duchess
would have to be a woman of impeccable breeding and character.

"How misnamed Angela is," His Grace said. "There is
nothing angelic about her. She is selfish, spoiled, extravagant, and incapable of running a household. What a dreadful
wife she would make. She would have my home—and God
knows it is less than satisfactory already—in a shambles
within a fortnight."

Although Charlie would have added a few even more
unflattering adjectives to this description, he thought that all
in all the duke had summed up Lady Bradwell's character
with notable accuracy.

"Furthermore," His Grace said, "Angela would make
an even worse mother. Children bore her, and she would
think that once she had given birth to them, her maternal
duties were finished. I will not inflict such a mother on my
children."

"But who, pray tell before I die of curiosity, is their
mother going to be?" Charlie demanded, fidgeting impatiently on the divan. The toe of his well-polished black
leather boot bumped the forgotten snuffbox, and he bent
over to retrieve it.

"I don't know," the duke said.

Charlie's jaw fell, and he very nearly dropped his snuffbox a second time. "You're hoaxing me, Alex!" Only

Charlie and one or two of Alexander's bolder inamoratas dared use the diminutive of his name, for he was a man of redoubtable consequence. The duke's reputation for reckless courage had been enhanced by the several successful duels he had fought and by his penchant for riding alone at night across notorious Hounslow Heath and Fincheley Common. He was utterly unconcerned by the danger of highwaymen, which made other gentlemen surround themselves with armed guards.

His Grace, when he cared, could be enormously charming, but on other occasions his tongue could be as biting as his blade. He was noted for his exquisite taste in everything from wine and women to food and furnishings. It was a coup for hostesses to have him at their parties, but his acceptance was enough to induce the vapors, so great was their anxiety at entertaining this witty perfectionist.

But Charlie saw a face very different from the one his brother showed to the world. He knew Alex to be exceedingly generous, kind, and concerned to those people whom he cared for. Charlie had discerned, as others had not, that neither the sincere nor the pitiful need fear Alex's tongue. He saved his barbed wit for puffed-up fools whose pretensions, unwarranted conceit, or unctuous hypocrisy made them ridiculous in Alex's keen gray eyes.

"Stop teasing me, Alex," Charlie pleaded. "Who is your bride-to-be?"

"I wish I knew." The duke sat down at his writing table. Although it was the dead of winter, a silver vase amid the clutter held two yellow hothouse roses. His Grace especially liked flowers and had them about at all times. "I know only that the wedding must be soon and that the bride must possess a substantial fortune."

Charlie, who knew in what contempt his brother held fortune hunters, was struck dumb.

"I am up to my eyebrows in debt," the duke explained.

"If I am to save the House of Hadleigh from disgrace, I fear I have no choice but to barter my title for a fortune."

The disgust and anguish in his voice told Charlie that Alex was torn between his responsibility to protect the family honor and repugnance at the idea of such a marriage. Charlie hastened to comfort the duke with sentiments that he himself, with his romantic heart, abhorred. "Why do you look so unhappy with yourself? Almost everyone in our circle marries for money or advantage—and preferably both."

"I am filled with revulsion that money must be any consideration at all."

"Your noble sentiments are not widely shared by my acquaintances, Alex. What did you hope to marry for?"

"For a wife of liveliness and breeding to be my companion, to bear my children, and to run my household smoothly and efficiently. If I must marry, I infinitely prefer it to be a woman of warmth, understanding, and intelligence who will be devoted to her husband and her children."

Charlie grinned. "It seems to me your wife must possess quite a few attributes other than a fortune." Alex's real problem, in Charlie's opinion, was that none of his many affairs had ever truly engaged his heart. The duke had embarked upon each amour lightly, with the certainty that it would soon end. And it had—always at his initiative.

Charlie, who knew his brother better than anyone, blamed Alex's fickleness on his having succeeded to his title while still in his teens. Since then—he was now thirty-three—every eligible young lady in London and her mama had been frantic to shackle him. But he had remained stubbornly single, taking his pleasure with his light of loves, who were inevitably beautiful and fascinating.

It was easy for Charlie to see why women doted on the duke. Not only were there his title and position, but he was intimidating in looks, stature, and personality. Charlie thought of the eight previous dukes whose portraits lined the long gallery at Mistelay, Stratford's country estate. None had been as handsome as the current titleholder. Charlie, who was a shorter, stouter version of his elder brother, thicker of face and feature, might have been jealous, but he was not. He had worshiped Alex, nine years his senior, since he had been a toddler.

Charlie fiddled absently with the catch of the snuffbox. Much as he loved the duke, he thought that if a woman undazzled by His Grace's title and charm had rejected him with a sharp trimming, it would have done him a world of good. But none had.

Charlie stared down at the lid of his snuffbox, which was set with a miniature of their late mother. She had not been a beauty, but she had been vivacious and candid. The blunt-talking dowager could be counted on to give her eldest son a setdown when he became arrogant, and he had loved her for it. Indeed, the duke had preferred her quick wit and lively intelligence to all the beauties in London.

But Charlie kept his speculations to himself. Aloud, he said, "I thought beauty and passion rather than conduct and intelligence were your major prerequisites in a woman, Alex."

His Grace shrugged. "One looks for very different things in a wife than in a mistress. One is permanent, the other temporary. Beauty and passion are easily found outside marriage."

"I pity the poor woman you marry," Charlie said.

"Why?" Alexander asked in genuine surprise. "I shall treat her with the greatest kindness, respect, and courtesy. She shall want for nothing."

"Except your love."

The duke's eyes gleamed with teasing humor. "But she shall have me. A great many women would have been delighted to settle for only that."

How true, Charlie thought. He remembered the many applications that he had made to Alex for payment of huge gambling debts and other extravagances. The duke had settled them all cheerfully until very recently, when he had warned his brother that his generosity in such matters was wearing thin. Now Charlie understood why, and he was conscience-stricken. "It's my fault you're in such straits, isn't it, Alex? My gambling debts have reduced you to this?"

The duke gave him an affectionate smile. "No, Charlie. The crop failures the past two years have contributed. And so have I."

"You don't gamble."

"My weakness, as you well know, is women."

It was true that Alex was famous for indulging his lady loves. Only two weeks ago, Charlie had seen Roxanne Sykes, the famous actress who had been Alex's convenient two years before, proudly wearing the fabulous ruby necklace he had given her.

Charlie opened his snuffbox, and a strong scent of attar of roses wafted up from it.

His Grace sniffed the fragrance. "I am delighted to detect that you have switched to Macouba."

"You were right, Alex, as you generally are in everything. Masulipatam is too strongly flavored." Charlie took a pinch from the box. "By the way, I am dining tomorrow night with Gilfred Sillsby. Now, there is a true fortune hunter. He has chased after every female in England who has an income of more than ten thousand a year."

"Good Lord, Charlie, he is such a pretentious fool and a terrible bore in the bargain. Why would you dine with him?"

"Curiosity. He left London a se'enight ago saying he was on his way to make an heiress of vast fortune his betrothed. Her father had already consented to the match. Sillsby indicated that she had reached the advanced age where she would welcome any prospect, so of course she would be overjoyed by so fine a figure as himself.''

"I see Sillsby is as modest as ever," the duke said with a sardonic chuckle. "Such a fine figure, indeed. Plump as a piglet. And those ridiculous frock coats he wears. Their shoulders are padded to twice the width of his own, and his waist is corseted more tightly than a woman's.''

"He is very proud of those coats," Charlie said gravely. "He assured me that they gave him the torso of an Adonis.''

Alexander laughed. "And what do those even sillier collars that he wears give him other than a stiff neck? They are starched to the hardness of a plaster cast, and the points extend so ridiculously high that they conceal half his face.'' Alexander's face turned somber. "To think that is the kind of man whose ranks I am forced to join." The duke's tone was weighted with repugnance. "Who is the unfortunate lady he means to wed?''

"I wish I knew. That is why I am having dinner with him. He would not confess her name until he returned to London with their betrothal sealed.'' Charlie gave his brother a quizzical look. "I suppose you have drawn up a list of prospective brides.''

The duke shrugged helplessly. "You know that I have never in my life paid the slightest attention to the size of a woman's fortune.''

"Come with me to Sillsby's. I was to bring George Keastley with me, but he's abed with the influenza. I'll bring you instead.''

Alexander shuddered at the prospect. "I cannot abide Sillsby.''

Charlie rose to his feet and slipped his snuffbox into his pocket. "But you will find him useful. He knows every eligible heiress in England and the size of her fortune to the nearest shilling. As a bonus, we'll learn the identity of the poor heiress whom he has snagged.''

CHAPTER 2

It was not an heiress, however, but Gilfred Sillsby's plan that was snagged.

As he prepared to return to London after a week at Greycote, the country home of Lord Landane, Sillsby was confounded by the reception he had received from his lordship's daughter, Diana, the heiress whom Sillsby had been so confident of marrying.

Landane, who generally resided in London while his daughter lived at Greycote, had accompanied Sillsby to the country. Upon their arrival, both father and suitor had been disconcerted to find Mary Prentice, the daughter of a parson who had once held the living in the nearby village, staying with Diana. Unfortunately for Sillsby, Miss Prentice had attached herself to her hostess with the tenacity of a leech, and not even the broadest of hints could dislodge her. It had been dashedly awkward trying to fix Miss Landane's interest with Miss Prentice constantly at her side.

Finally, last night Lord Landane had had to order his daughter to see Sillsby privately so that he could make his offer to her. Although he showered Miss Landane with effusive compliments that were so patently false they all but stuck in his craw as he uttered them, she had the effrontery to laugh at him.

If she had not been the most vexingly stupid, sullen female Sillsby had ever met, she would have jumped at the offer of such a splendid man as he. She, on the other hand, had absolutely nothing to recommend her except her magnificent fortune. Everything about her was dull, from hair the color of scrub water and pulled back in an ugly knot to sickly yellow skin and defective eyes behind ugly wire spectacles.

He thought of the portrait of her mother, the late Lady

Landane, that hung in a small sitting room downstairs. He was amazed that such a lovely creature could have produced so ugly a daughter.

Sillsby would have been far more amazed could he have seen Miss Landane at that moment. For she bore a striking resemblance to the portrait of her mother except that the daughter was prettier. She was sitting in a blue wrapper before her dressing table, brushing out thick waves of fine golden hair that shimmered in the light as they cascaded down her back. Her flawless skin had the soft delicacy and color of white rose petals.

When Mary Prentice entered the room, Diana's lively blue eyes sparkled like rare gemstones as she gestured to a chair beside her own. "Do join me, Mary."

Settling in the chair, Mary grinned at her friend. "What a pleasure to see the real Diana again."

Diana's eyes gleamed, and she gurgled with irrepressible laughter. "Yes, it must be a great relief for all who must look upon me when I abandon my disguise."

"I do not see how you can bear to don it." Mary shuddered. "That vile concoction you use to turn your skin yellow is repulsive."

Diana put her hairbrush down on the dressing table, cluttered with jars of disgusting-looking potions. "The powder I use to dull my hair is worse, because it is so difficult to remove."

Mary pointed to a small jar filled with an oozy black substance. "What do you use this dreadful mess for?"

"To draw the dark circles under my eyes."

"So that is how you manage to look as though you had not slept in weeks," Mary said. She noticed Diana's worn blue wrapper and how piled high with petticoats the basket of mending next to the dressing table was. What irony, Mary thought, that the heiress to one of England's greatest fortunes could not afford a decent dressing gown and new petticoats. But under the terms of the will left by Sir John Wakely, Diana's maternal grandfather, she could not inherit his money until she married. Then the huge fortune would be placed under her husband's control.

It had been her grandfather's way of making certain that his despised son-in-law, Lord Landane, could not get his hands on some of the money. But it had also left Diana, until she married, entirely dependent on her ramshackle, dissipated father, whose own finances were highly precarious. His only interest in his daughter, as far as Mary could see, was to wed her to whatever fortune hunter would agree to give his lordship a portion of her fortune. Meanwhile, he expected Diana to run Greycote on a mere pittance.

"I cannot fathom, Diana, why your grandfather did not provide you with a small stipend so that you could set up your own modest household independent of your father until you married and claimed the full inheritance."

"Grandpa did not because he knew how much I would despise being dependent on my father."

Mary frowned. "I do not understand."

"Grandpapa wished above all else for me to be suitably wed, and he knew how opposed I was to marriage. But he also knew how repugnant it would be to me to be dependent on my father. I am certain Grandpapa thought that I would rather take a husband. So he sought by the terms of his will to persuade me to marry." Diana chuckled. "As you can see, his strategy failed."

Mary pointed to a pair of heavy wire-rimmed spectacles, another part of Diana's disguise, lying amid the jars on the dressing table. "Are they merely plain glass?"

Diana nodded and made a face. "How I hate them. They pinch my nose dreadfully. But hardest of all is having to hold my tongue and act like a sullen half-wit."

"Indeed, that must be an enormous challenge," Mary exclaimed. In fact, she was quite astonished that Diana, who was as lively and quick-witted as she was pretty, could manage to carry off her charade so convincingly. "Is your wretched disguise worth it?"

"But of course it is!" Diana's infectious laugh bubbled up. Its clear, melodic tones reminded Mary of the bells that rang in the steeple of her father's church. "It has routed even the most determined of fortune hunters that my father has tried to peddle me to—except Sillsby."

"What?" Mary exclaimed. "I cannot believe that he actually made you an offer? Why, when he first saw you, the look of horror on his face was hilarious."

"You see how exceedingly desperate he is." Diana's laughter bubbled up again. "Oh, Mary, if only you could have heard the outrageous compliments that he paid me. Even such a toad-eater as he nearly choked trying to get out such lies." Diana, who had a remarkable gift for mimicry, imitated Sillsby's effusive, nasal voice: "My dear Miss Landane, what beautiful coloring you have. Quite out of the ordinary."

"Quite out of a jar," Mary said, shaking with laughter at the unerring accuracy of Diana's imitation. "I cannot believe even he could dissemble so."

"But that was only the beginning. To hear him, you would have thought that I was Venus herself. It was so difficult not to dissolve in laughter. Especially when he tried to kiss my hand in that silly starched collar of his, which forces him to hold his head up as though he were caught in a vise."

Diana thrust her nose up and her head back at the awkward angle that Sillsby's collar dictated. Jumping up from her seat, she imitated his futile efforts to bend his encased neck over her hand. "Then he tried to bow from the waist, but his corset stays would not permit that, either. He laces himself so tightly that I cannot imagine how he can breathe."

"Nor I," Mary agreed. Previously, she had faulted Diana's mother, embittered by her own experience, for having filled Diana with unjustified dread of marriage in general and fear of fortune hunters in particular. But having met Sillsby, Mary was now more appreciative of Diana's apprehensions.

"The best came when he made his offer." Diana's eyes danced with laughter. "He got his words twisted around, and instead of asking me for the honor of my hand, he said he was doing me the honor of marrying me. Of course, that is exactly what he thought, but it was not what he meant to say."

"What did you do?"

"I am afraid I could stand it no longer. I burst out laughing."

"How did he react to your rejection?"

Diana laughed. "Oh, he was quite livid. He told me that anyone as long in the tooth as I was should be ecstatic to have received such a fine offer as his. Furthermore, he would marry me whether I wished it or not, since my father had given his permission."

"What did you do?"

"I informed him more fully of the terms of my grandfather's will." Diana picked up a petticoat from her basket of mending and examined the tear in one of its ruffles. "You see, it stipulated that the trustee, Stanley Pearce must approve my husband, or I cannot inherit. I told Sillsby that both he and my father are utter fools to think that Mr. Pearce will ever give his approval to my marrying Sillsby or anyone else of his ilk. That information put an instant end to his suit."

"But if that is the case, you do not need your dreadful disguise," Mary protested. "You are quite safe from fortune hunters."

"Safe from only the obvious ones. My greatest fear is that someone of consequence who is acceptable to Mr. Pearce will make me an offer." Diana opened her sewing basket and selected a needle and thread from it. "The will specifically states that only Mr. Pearce's approval, not my own, is required. Should that happen, it would be very much more difficult for me to resist."

"But perhaps it would be a man that you yourself would want to marry."

"Nonsense." Diana's eyes flashed with angry determination. "I will never give a man control over me so that he may treat me as miserably as my father treated my mother."

Mary had only small sympathy for the late Lady Landane, a willful, spoiled beauty who had never accepted the husband imposed upon her. True, her marriage had been disastrous. But Mary's own father and everyone else who had known the Landanes were of the strong belief that both parties had been at fault.

However, Diana had heard only her mother's side, and that she had heard endlessly. Lord Landane had banished his wife and daughter to Greycote when Diana had been a toddler, while he himself had remained in London, never visiting his estranged wife and daughter. Diana had known no world but Greycote until she was in her teens. Then her mother had gone to live on the shores of Lake Geneva, taking Diana with her. Later, when the pair had returned to London, Landane had permitted them to stay with Wakely, under whose roof Diana had remained after her mother's death until Wakely, too, died, four years earlier. So Diana and her father had been virtual strangers to each other until the terms of her grandfather's will had forced her back beneath his lordship's roof, to the mutual dismay of father and daughter. Since then, their relationship had remained frosty. Diana stayed at Greycote, while her father resided mostly in London.

It was fortunate, Mary thought, that Diana was so well liked and her father so hated in the area that no one would dream of betraying to him the remarkable transformation his daughter underwent whenever he appeared at Greycote. "Since your disguise is so important to you, Diana, why have you abandoned it this morning while your father and Sillsby are still here?"

"They leave this morning, and I said my farewells to them last night." Diana had threaded the needle and was applying it with quick skill to the torn petticoat. "When Sillsby made his offer, he told me with great self-importance that he must be back in London tonight because he is to dine with Lord Charles Hadleigh, the duke of Stratford's brother. He meant to impress me by throwing out Stratford's name, never suspecting that I consider him the most odious of men."

"Odious? But I have heard that he is irresistible to women."

"Only when he chooses to be," Diana said dryly. "In my case, he did not so choose. Fortunately, our acquaintance was very brief, only long enough for me to form a lasting dislike of him."

"Since Sillsby is leaving, I must depart, too," Mary said. She hated to leave. Diana was such fun to be with, and she had turned Greycote into as cheerful and comfortable a house as Mary had ever seen. Mary would happily have stayed for several more weeks. Unfortunately, however, she had long been committed to a month-long visit with her aunt in Bath that was to begin four days hence.

Diana dropped the petticoat she was mending into her lap, reached out, and took Mary's hands in her own. "I cannot thank you enough, Mary, for rushing to me on such short notice. I do not know what I would have done without you here to help frustrate Sillsby's suit. I fear Mrs. Cottam is of no help at all in such situations."

"Nor in any other, I would imagine," Mary said tartly. She found Diana's elderly companion-chaperone—a timid, helpless widow given to nervous spasms at the flimsiest provocation and devoted to the most inconsequential gossip—tedious. Mary could not imagine how anyone as lively and independent as Diana could tolerate Mrs. Cottam. "Surely you could find a more congenial companion."

Diana was horrified by the suggestion. "But she is penniless and has nowhere else to go. Besides, she is really a dear woman."

"But don't you find it terribly lonely here with only her for company."

"I daresay it is harder now that so many of my old friends are gone." Diana resumed mending her petticoat. "Elizabeth Whorton, who was like my sister, married and moved away years ago, of course. She has two little girls now. And her dear mother died last year. I miss you and your family. But I still have Elizabeth's brother, George, and her father. And I have my painting."

"Does your father come here often?"

"Normally, only once a year for a fortnight in the summer. His coming like this in January is unheard of." Diana grinned at her friend. "Of course, we know his reason."

Mary smiled back. "I hope he does not find another eager fortune hunter to present to you during the next month while I am in Bath, for I will not be able to come to your aid."

"Father will not be back until summer. He assured me quite emphatically last night how delighted he was that he would not have to set eyes on me again until then."

CHAPTER 3

When Gilfred Sillsby's dinner guests arrived that night, he was horrified to discover that instead of George Keastley, Lord Charles Hadleigh had brought his brother, the formidable duke of Stratford, whose epicurean tastes for only the very best in food, wine, and women were famous.

While the dinner would be perfectly adequate for the duke's amiable, easygoing brother, who never seemed to notice the niceties of table or bottle, it would never do for the notoriously fastidious duke. Sillsby hastily whispered instructions to his footman that caused no end of consternation and frantic endeavor in his kitchen, then sent a servant hurrying to the cellar for the very finest bottle of wine he possessed. He had put it away for an exalted occasion, such as his betrothal to an heiress who could afford to replenish it after their marriage.

If only Lord Charles had given Sillsby advance warning so that he could have ordered a fit meal prepared, he would have been honored to have the duke at his table, even overjoyed.

Well, perhaps not overjoyed, for Sillsby was awed and a little frightened of the arrogant Stratford. Still, it was quite a feather to snag the duke to one's table. It was well known that he rejected ten invitations for each one he accepted. Sillsby already was planning to use the phrase "When the duke of Stratford dined at my house recently" as soon as he found another heiress to court.

The thought of how the phrase would enhance his consequence in the eyes of that awed young lady almost—but not quite—offset his nervousness about what lay immediately ahead. Slowly, with all the happy expectation of a man being taken to the guillotine, Sillsby led his guests to the dining parlor. The duke, elegant as always, stood more than half a head taller than Sillsby. Although Sillsby was particularly proud of his frock coat, with his wide padded shoulders and nipped-in waist, and of his cream silk waistcoat with blue-and-silver embroidery, which was his best, he felt shabby beside the duke. It was not that His Grace affected the flashy style of a dandy. His forest-green coat over a pale-green corded silk waistcoat achieved its elegant effect by perfect tailoring and the most expensive of fabrics.

As they sat down at the table, Sillsby signaled the footman to fill the wineglasses from the fine bottle of wine. He hoped the duke would notice its excellent vintage, although it was hard to imagine anything impressing His Grace's cold gray eyes. Nevertheless, Sillsby had more faith in the wine than he did in any dish that could possibly emerge from his kitchen.

Charlie picked up his glass. "Shall we toast your betrothal?"

Sillsby flushed with indignation as he remembered the reception his offer had received. "No," he snapped, taking a large gulp of wine, "I am not betrothed."

"My condolences," the duke said dryly, lifting his glass and his arched right eyebrow simultaneously.

Quivering with hurt pride, Sillsby responded surlily, "Congratulations on my escape would be more in order."

The duke's right eyebrow again arched quizzingly. "The lady was not rich enough?"

"Oh, she was rich enough." Sillsby nodded to the servant to begin serving the soup and to replenish the wine, having already drained his own glass. "She was quite the richest heiress I know of. Her income alone exceeds a hundred thousand a year."

Interest flickered in the duke's eyes at this staggering sum.

Charlie gave an impressed gasp. "I am surprised a

woman of such surpassing fortune was not snatched up long ago."

Sillsby gave Charlie a sour look. "You would not be surprised had you met her. She has nothing to recommend her, nothing at all; no beauty, no liveliness, no charm." Angrily, he lifted a spoonful of the leek soup to his mouth and discovered to his horror that he was serving an exceedingly gray and lumpy concoction to so noted a gourmet as the duke of Stratford. This embarrassment coupled with that of Diana Landane's rejection unleashed his tongue. "Furthermore, she is already long in the tooth. You would think at the age of four and twenty such an antidote would be delighted to accept an offer from a man far less pleasing than I, but she had the gall to laugh in my face."

Stratford looked up in sudden interest from his soup, which he had been contemplating with some fascination. "Laughed at you, did she? Who is this ridiculous creature?"

Sillsby had a fleeting impression that His Grace was mocking him. "Lord Landane's daughter."

"What?" The duke's right eyebrow shot up. "The daughter of a third-rate baron laughed at you?"

His host nodded. Although the duke's tone was sympathetic, Sillsby could not shake the feeling that His Grace was mocking him.

"You said she was a great heiress," the duke continued, "but her father is not even well fixed."

Sillsby, seeing that the duke had put down his spoon and had no intention of eating the offending soup, hastily motioned to the servant to remove the dishes and bring the next course. "Her money comes from her maternal grandfather, Sir John Wakely."

"The crown's own banker. Certainly there was none richer than he," the duke observed.

The fish, a sole overcooked to the toughness of lean beefsteak, was served. The duke tested it. A glint of repugnance flashed in his eye, and he reached for his wineglass. "Wakely has been dead some years. I would that Lord Landane would have made a sizable dent by now even in so huge a fortune."

"Can't get his hands on it." Sillsby drained his wine and motioned to the servant to refill the glasses again. As the wine was being poured, Sillsby outlined the terms of Wakely's will. "So until she marries to Stanley Pearce's satisfaction, the huge income from the estate continues to be plowed back into it, piling up still more capital and an even larger income."

"Wakely left his granddaughter in good hands," the duke said approvingly. "Old Pearce is as shrewd a man as can be found anywhere."

Sillsby noted with dismay that the bottle of good wine had been emptied and the servant was refilling the duke's glass from an inferior bottle. The host prayed His Grace would not notice.

Leaning back in his chair, the duke examined Sillsby thoughtfully. "So Landane agreed to your marrying his daughter in return for your paying over a portion of her fortune to him once you gained control of it."

The duke's quick perception of the situation discomforted Sillsby. He hastily signaled for the removal of the untouched plate of fish from before His Grace and the serving of the next dish, a vol-au-vent of chicken. "That was only part of the reason," Sillsby said.

The duke took a sip of wine from his newly refilled glass, stared at it with considerable surprise, and hastily set it down. "Pray what was the rest of the reason?"

"Landane plans to marry again, and he wants to dislodge his daughter from Greycote before he brings his bride there."

The duke's right eyebrow formed a question mark. "Who is the bride?"

"Sir Randolph Owsley's daughter, Isabel."

"But she must be younger than Landane's own daughter," Stratford said.

Sillsby nodded and drained his wineglass. Although the wine did have a slightly vinegary taste, he decided it was really quite good when one got used to it. He noted uneasily, however, that the duke was not drinking his. Nor was he eating the vol-au-vent. "There's no fool like an old fool, Your Grace, and Landane's quite lost his silly head over little Isabel."

"I cannot imagine why. She gives every sign of being as great a shrew as her mother." Stratford tapped the tips of his fingers together thoughtfully. "Such a marriage will not improve Landane's finances. Isabel is the youngest of four daughters, her dowry will be minuscule, and she is a spoiled brat whose only talent is for extravagance."

Sillsby made a stab at the vol-au-vent. It skidded half off his plate. He tried again with greater care, but it was so tough it defied conquering.

"Have you ever met this Miss Landane?" Charlie asked his brother.

"I have no recollection of ever doing so," the duke replied.

"Why have I never seen her in London?" Charlie asked his host.

"She's something of a recluse. She detests London and prefers the country."

"Has she nothing at all to recommend her?" Charlie asked.

"Nothing," Sillsby replied with conviction. "Except she does run a most comfortable and efficient house with an excellent kitchen," he added wistfully as he contemplated his sorry table.

Interest again flickered in the duke's gray eyes.

Seeing it, Charlie asked hastily, "What other heiresses are about this season, Sillsby?"

The host shook his head morosely. "Worst crop ever. After Miss Landane, there's only Miss Mackay and Lord Tucker's daughter. Neither has an income above eight thousand."

As Stratford and his brother rode home in the duke's polished, high-sprung coach with the ducal crest on the door, Charlie said, "If you must marry for money, I guess the best of the lot is Lord Tucker's daughter.

The duke's face was inscrutable in the flickering light of the carriage lamp. "I should think my title is worth considerably more than eight thousand a year," he said sardonically.

"But at least she is a pretty young thing."

"As well as a simpering bore whose most profound thought is whether her curls are properly arranged. At least Miss Landane had the good sense to laugh at that posturing fool Sillsby."

Charlie was aghast. "Surely you are not considering Miss Landane."

The duke shrugged. "She is of excellent breeding. Wakely was related to half the best families in England. Landane is a fool, but he is of good lineage, especially on his mother's side.

"But if even half of what Sillsby says is true—"

"I suspect that Sillsby's wounded pride led him to exaggerate. Even he admits Miss Landane runs an exemplary household, which is an attraction in itself." A grim smile played on the duke's lips. "Besides, you underestimate how desperate my situation is."

"There has to be some other way, Alex. Cut your expenses to the bone. Mistelay, for example. You have not been there in months. It is foolish to keep a full staff there.''

"I don't, Charlie. There's only a caretaker and his wife. That's one reason I don't go there.''

"I had no idea," Charlie gasped. Then, as was his nature, he tried to find a brighter side. "Since you aren't using it, perhaps you could sell off some of the furnishings.''

"I already have. That's the other reason I don't go there. I fear that you would be shocked and heartsick if you saw our ancestral home now. Nor is it just the house. Without a large staff of gardeners to maintain the grounds, they have deteriorated into a jungle that I am ashamed to have anyone see.''

Charlie, who knew how much his brother loved Mistelay and its gardens, reached out to touch his arm consolingly.

"How far into dun territory are you?''

"I have cornered the kingdom. What is worse, my creditors have sniffed ruin and are marshaling to pick me clean. Only an infusion of great sums will keep the House of Hadleigh afloat past summer.''

"So it's as bad as all that?''

The duke nodded, his face set in grim lines.

"Hadn't you better at least meet Miss Landane before you think of marriage?''

The duke's sardonic humor was restored. "If she is as dreadful an antidote as Sillsby maintains, I would prefer to postpone that moment as long as possible.''

Charlie knew Alex was funning, but he foresaw disaster. "If she is as dreadful as Sillsby said, I cannot imagine you married to her.''

"Nor will I be. She must have more to recommend her than just her fortune, no matter how large it is. But I shall at least look her over.''

"What if she is averse to a match with you?''

Alexander looked at him as if he had quite lost his mind. "My dear Charlie, she will be delighted at the prospect of becoming the duchess of Stratford on whatever terms I dictate. I shall see to that.''

Alex would, too, Charlie thought. There had never been a woman yet who could resist the duke when he set about to win her heart. She would be like melting butter in Alex's hands within a day of their acquaintance.

CHAPTER 4

Five days after Lord Landane and Sillsby had left Greycote, his lordship returned without warning. Diana was filled with consternation and foreboding. She was slightly relieved to learn that her father was alone. At least he was not accompanied by another fortune hunter. But her apprehension heightened when he immediately sent for her. Hastily, she applied her disguise and presented herself to him in the library.

He was in ill humor. ''I said I wished to see you at once. You have kept me waiting twenty minutes.''

''I was not dressed,'' she fibbed. ''Why have you come back? When you left, you said you would not return until summer.''

''I changed my mind,'' her father replied. Both his face and his body had been thickened and coarsened by years of drink and dissipation, but he still retained some of the youthful handsomeness that had made him vain as a peacock. ''Guests are coming to join us.''

She stared at her father as though he had taken leave of his senses. "Guests! Who would want to come here in January when it is so cold and ugly?"

"Lord and Lady Owsley and their youngest daughter, Isabel, arrive day after tomorrow." He paused, studying her. "And the duke of Stratford comes tomorrow afternoon for two nights."

"The duke of Stratford here! At Greycote?" Diana could not have been more astonished if the Prince of Wales himself were coming. The arrogant Stratford was notorious for rejecting invitations even to the best houses. She could not imagine him so lowering his consequence as to visit the insignificant country home of a minor baron. "Surely you are joking."

"No." His lordship fairly preened over this social triumph. "He is stopping here on his way to visit his sister, the marchioness of Harland, at her country home."

"Why stop here?" Diana persisted.

"I am not in the habit of asking the motives of men who desire to visit me. It is an enormous honor to have him. I pray you make certain that he does not regret his decision to stop. Or is that too much to ask from you?"

Diana bristled at the unfair jibe. Although she kept unobtrusively in the background during her father's summer house parties, she made certain that his guests enjoyed the warmest hospitality. Their every comfort was attended to, the food was superb, and the entertainment was varied. So successful were her efforts that many a guest looked forward to a repeat invitation to Greycote even though he had found his host a drunken bore.

Only Mrs. Cottam knew with what limited resources Diana worked her magic. Landane gave Diana only a trifling sum on which to run Greycote. That she did so successfully was a tribute to her extraordinary management skills, to which her father was oblivious. Still, she hated the constant struggle to make ends meet.

And now, much as she might dislike Stratford, she had no intention of providing him with anything but the very best that Greycote was capable of. She remembered how widely quoted were his witty criticisms of certain pretentious hostesses. If he expected to amuse himself—and all of London—by recounting the deficiencies he had found at Greycote, he would be sorely disappointed.

Diana issued a series of orders that soon had the household in a flurry of activity. Furniture, already spotless, was dusted and polished again. The best bedchamber was aired and prepared. Diana revised her menus, substituting dishes that threatened to bankrupt her budget.

Diana overslept the next morning and awoke to the news, delivered by Mrs. Cottam, that Lord Landane already had ridden out to meet Stratford on the road from London and escort him personally to Greycote.

Diana blushed with embarrassment. "Does Father fear the duke might change his mind at the last moment and bypass Greycote? Father is excessively nervous over Stratford's visit."

"So am I," confessed Mrs. Cottam, a plump dumpling of a woman with white hair and a well-wrinkled face. Diana noted with amusement that in expectation of the Duke's arrival, Mrs. Cottam was wearing her prettiest morning dress, a sprigged muslin with a satin ribbon at the waist that she saved for only the grandest occasions. Her ample body had been corseted into rigid and unnatural submission. "What a great honor it is for His Grace to stop here."

"But why would he deign to do so?" Diana asked. She rose from her bed and slipped into her blue wrapper. "This is not at all the sort of grand establishment he condescends to honor with his presence."

Mrs. Cottam's plump hands fluttered with excitement. "For once I shall have something to write my sister." Mrs. Cottam was addicted to gossip and to wildly improbable romantic novels. Greycote had nothing to offer her in the way of scandalous gossip. This void was filled by her sister, Mrs. Wise, who lived in London and sent frequent, many-paged letters of tiny, closely spaced handwriting that chronicled every scrap of scandal or gossip extant in London.

Mrs. Wise, whom Diana considered singularly misnamed, never failed to pass on the most improbable on-dits as the gospel truth. Mrs. Cottam would chatter so incessantly about the contents of the letters that Diana had come to dread their arrival.

"My sister will be so awed and envious when she hears that we have actually entertained the celebrated duke." Stratford's scandalous affairs had been a favorite topic in Mrs. Wise's letters, and Mrs. Cottam's faded eyes glittered with excitement. "He is a notorious rake. Even Harriette Wilson, the most sought-after Cyprian of them all, was quite mad about him. And that actress Sykes—the one who was so beautiful Prinny threatened to kill himself over her—was so devastated that she could not perform for three months after the duke left her. His current favorite, Lady Bradwell, is reputed to be quite the greatest beauty of the day, but of course, the duke's convenients are always famous for their beauty."

Diana, anxious to avoid a detailed bibliography of the duke's many love affairs, hastily interjected, "There has to be some reason for Stratford's visit. I wonder what it is father hopes to gain by it."

The sudden hopeful gleam of an incurable romantic shone in Mrs. Cottam's eyes. "Perhaps he hopes the duke will offer for you."

The thought was so ludicrous to Diana that she burst out laughing. "Don't be silly. Stratford is so arrogant and full of his own consequence that he finds even the most desirable women beneath his touch. Nor," she added with sudden vehemence, "can I think of anything more dreadful than to be married to that arrogant rake. Not that there is the slightest chance he would notice me. Father has windmills in his head if he thinks he could possibly interest Stratford in a poor drab like me."

Diana walked into her dressing room and sat down before the table loaded with jars of makeup.

"But you are not a poor drab," Mrs. Cottam protested, following her. "You only pretend to be."

She watched in horror as Diana dipped into one of the jars and began applying its ugly yellow contents to her delicate white skin. "Surely you are not going to wear that when the duke is here. You will disgust him!"

"Perhaps then he will cut short his stay."

"Is he on his way to Mistelay?" Mrs. Cottam asked. "They say it is the handsomest place Inigo Jones ever designed."

"It is not just the house that is supposed to be beautiful, but the gardens, the furnishings, and the paintings." These things excited Diana, who was an artist herself, far more than jewels or gowns. "The long gallery is lined with old masters—Rubens, Titians, Rembrandts, Van Dykes." Diana spoke the names with reverence. "The saloon is filled with cabinets of Sevres, Meissen, and Chinese porcelains. Oh, how I would love to see Mistelay."

"Perhaps if you would try to fix the duke's interest," Mrs. Cottam began timidly, but she was cut short by Diana's scornful response.

"Of all the men I met in London, I disliked him by far the most. He is so arrogant and full of his own consequence."

"But my sister says he is exceedingly handsome and charming."

"To be sure, he is excessively handsome, and he can be charming when he wishes to exert himself." Having turned her skin a sickly yellow, Diana dipped into another jar and began filling in dark circles beneath her eyes.

"How did you meet him?"

"It was during my wretched season in London years ago. I suspect that it was Grandpapa's secret dream that somehow he might marry me to Stratford." Diana stared into the mirror, surveying with satisfaction the ugly circles beneath her eyes. "Nothing would have pleased Grandpapa more than for me to marry such an illustrious title. After much maneuvering, he managed to get the duke seated beside me at a dinner of Lady Hardy's."

Diana attacked her hair angrily with her brush. Her cheeks still flushed with embarrassment when she remembered that night. "The duke was in rare form and had everyone at the table quite dissolved in laughter with his caustic wit. He hardly spoke to me. When I saw him at Almack's the next night, he did not recognize me."

"You won't be rude to him, will you?" Mrs. Cottam fingered her skirt nervously.

"Although it will gall me, I shall be polite." Diana applied a generous amount of gray powder to her blond hair and began brushing it in. "But I shall not be friendly."

Mrs. Cottam grimaced as Diana's shimmering blond hair slowly turned to a dull, grayish shade. "How can you do that to your beautiful hair? My dear child, you will discourage any man who might love you. Surely you must want to marry and have children."

In truth, Diana deeply longed for a husband who would love her for herself and not for her fortune and for a home and children of her own. But her mother had made her so suspicious of the motives of any man who might seek her hand that she was determined to remain a spinster rather than fall prey to a fortune hunter. "I would love to have children," she confessed a trifle wistfully.

"The problem is that you have never loved a man."

"That is not true." Diana pulled her now-ugly hair back

into a severe knot. "I was in love once." She thought of that summer when she had just turned sixteen and had been at Tante Germaine's villa on the shores of Lake Geneva. It had been Diana's first taste of life beyond Greycote, for she had been little more than a baby when Landane had banished his recalcitrant spouse there.

Although her mother had despised Greycote, Diana had loved it, thanks to Squire Whorton and his wife, whose land adjoined Greycote. They had taken pity on the lonely little girl and had made her as much a part of their boisterous, loving household as if she had been their own child. She had grown up regarding them as surrogate parents and their son, George, and his older sister, Elizabeth, as her brother and sister.

When Diana had been fifteen, Lord Landane had finally despaired of ever gaining his estranged wife's submission and had permitted her to leave Greycote if she would also leave England. So she had gone with Diana to live with Tante Germaine. Not that Germaine was Diana's real aunt, but rather Lady Landane's dearest friend since girlhood.

Germaine, who had inherited a considerable fortune from her father, had married a very wealthy French comte and was by then a refugee from the Revolution, which had sent her husband to the guillotine. She had surrounded herself with a dazzling circle of writers, thinkers, artists, actors, aristocrats, and musicians, all noted for their wit and talent.

They had entertained themselves with sparkling conversation, lovely musicales, and elaborate theatricals of their own devising. It was for the latter that Diana had learned the secrets of applying makeup to alter one's appearance drastically.

For the first time, Diana had understood fully why her mother, who had thrived on good conversation, company, and parties, had been so unhappy at Greycote and had hated her father so much for exiling her there from London.

Germaine's villa had also been a magnet for other French émigrés fleeing the Revolution. One of them had been Antoine, the twenty-three-year-old son of the comte de Couday, who had lost both his head and his vast holdings to the Revolution.

To Diana's young eyes, Antoine had been amusing, charming, and the handsomest young man she had ever seen. He had been her first and only love, and he had courted her assiduously. But Lady Landane had been convinced that he was a fortune hunter interested in nothing but the money that Diana would someday inherit from her grandfather.

Diana, however, had been too much in love to pay her mother any heed. She and Antoine had called themselves Heloise and Abelard, after those ill-starred medieval lovers, and had plotted, like their namesakes, a secret marriage. Somehow Mama had learned of their plan. The very next day she had set out for England, dragging her sobbing daughter with her.

Lady Landane took refuge in her father's house in London. Diana was certain that Grandpapa had paid Landane, who was always in need of money, to leave his wife in peace in London. She insisted that her daughter be launched into society during the next season. But by the time that season arrived, Mama was already dying.

Diane remembered her London season as the most miserable time of her life. First, there was the pain of watching her mama's slow and agonizing dying.

Second, Antoine had vindicated Lady Landane's opinion of him by eloping with Simone, Germaine's ugly, dull-witted, but very rich niece, two months after Diana and her mother had left Geneva. At first, Diana had refused to believe the news. It simply could not be true, she had insisted. Antoine loved her too much. It was true that Simone had been infatuated with Antoine, but he had had no interest in her. Indeed, he had often made fun of her to Diana.

But eventually confirmation of the wedding came from other sources, too, and Diana cried herself to sleep every night for weeks. Nor did Diana's mother miss an opportunity, thereafter, to impress upon her stunned, heartbroken daughter the horrible life that would await her should she wed a man attracted by her money.

The emotional devastation wrought in Diana by Antoine's perfidy and her mother's illness had caused her delicate white skin to erupt in hideous red blotches that made her look as though she were suffering from some dread disease. She had turned to food for consolation, eating herself into obesity. Her face became a fat moon, swallowing up the handsome planes that made it so striking. The large, lively blue eyes grew dull and sullen. All the gowns, resplendent with ruffles and tiers of skirts, that Mama had ordered for her when she was still slender made her look like a whale squeezed into a doll's dress.

Diana had not only been embarrassed by her appearance, but she had despised London. After the excitement and stimulation of Tante Germaine's brilliant crowd, she had been bored by the empty chatter of the ton and their dull assemblies. Diana had an unerring eye for the ridiculous, and she had longed for someone with whom she could share her amusement at the pompous pretensions and excesses of dress exhibited by the vain young dandies that crowded London drawing rooms. But her taste for deprecating humor and challenging conversation was ill appreciated by prospective suitors, who expected only beauty and innocuous coyness from eligible young ladies.

She was thankful that events conspired to deny her a second season. Mama's death at the beginning of the next season meant Diana spent it in mourning, never leaving her grandfather's house. By the following year, the smoke and fumes of London had driven her grandfather, stricken with consumption, from the city. She had gone with him to the country, where she lost the weight she had gained. Her eyes recaptured their sparkle, and her skin regained its unblemished softness. But she had learned well the value of ugliness in discouraging unwanted suitors.

After Grandpapa's death, she had come back to Greycote. There she was welcomed by Squire Whorton and his wife as if their own daughter had returned. She was quickly made to feel as if she were again one of their family.

Whenever her father, his boorish friends, or the fortune hunters he sponsored came to Greycote, she was careful to conceal her prettiness behind a mask of sallow makeup and thick glasses. None of them ever tempted her to discard her disguise. Nor were there suitors for her hand in the vicinity of Greycote. The only bachelor other than George Whorton, whom she regarded as a brother, was Squire Stevens's son. He, like his father, was a coarse, ignorant man who cared for nothing but his horses.

No, Diana thought sorrowfully as she put on a severe gray gown with high neck and long sleeves that did nothing to enhance her excellent figure and much to play up her now-sallow skin, she had no chance of making a satisfactory marriage.

Mrs. Cottam stared at her in horror. "Surely you are not going to wear that dreadful dress to greet the duke."

"But I am." Diana smiled sweetly. "The haughty, conceited duke of Stratford will find one female who does not dress to please him."

"But you are not even wearing stays." To Mrs. Cottam, stays were an article of faith, and any woman who was not corseted to the point of suffocation was all but naked. "The duke will be shocked."

Diana's eyes danced with laughter. "I sincerely hope so."

Mrs. Cottam was prevented from further entreaties by the announcement that Squire Whorton's son, George, had arrived. Diana smiled in delight at word of his unexpected visit. Since his sister, Elizabeth, had married and moved away, George had been her very closest friend in the world.

As Diana hurried into the little sitting room, where George awaited her, he rose from a chair upholstered in her own needlepoint. He was a rugged young man of two and twenty, square of face and features, with a wide smile that betrayed his imperturbable good humor. Diana greeted him with affection.

He looked at her quizzically. "Your father must be here."

"How did you know?"

He laughed. "You shatterbrain. From your appearance, of course. You could hardly have acquired such black circles beneath your eyes and contracted jaundice in the bargain since I saw you yesterday."

It was Diana's turn to laugh, but she quickly grew serious again. "Not only is Father here, but the duke of Stratford arrives this afternoon."

"You're joking! His Arrogance here? But he turns up his elegant nose at even the greatest houses."

"His Arrogance?"

"That's his nickname." George raised a cautioning hand. "Be careful of him. He is a dreadful rake."

Diana's eyes sparkled mischievously. "I hardly think that I am his type."

George hooted with laughter. "Not got up like that, you're not. His Arrogance will not come within fifty feet of you. His tastes run to the great beauties and the more exciting of the Cyprians. I don't envy you the job of making him comfortable. From what I hear, it would be easier to please Prinny himself than Stratford. In fact, when I was last in London, I heard His Arrogance had the gall to refuse

Prinny's invitation to Carleton House, complaining that the rooms were too overheated for his taste."

Diana moaned. "And I am supposed to entertain a man so haughty he dares to reject even the prince. I am certain he is stopping here only because he expects to amuse his friends with tales of an ill-run country house."

"He has a reputation for being less than kind to hostesses whose hospitality did not suit him."

Diana's lips tightened in determination. "I shall not be the butt of Stratford's wit." She seized George's arm. "You and your father must visit us tonight after dinner."

George looked appalled. "Spend an evening with His Arrogance? I should rather spend it in the stocks."

"George, please, you must help me. Can you imagine anything more disastrous than my father and Stratford together for an entire night?"

The expression on George's face told her he could not, but it took considerably more coaxing by Diana to secure his reluctant agreement to come.

"If I did not regard you as my own sister, Diana, I swear I would not let you subject me and my father to such a night. I imagine His Arrogance will be dripping with condescension, but I warn you, Diana, if he makes you or my father the target of that brutal wit of his, I shall not scruple to answer him in kind."

"I hope you will. I hope you give him a great setdown, for he is most deserving."

George turned to leave, then stopped and pulled a letter from his pocket. "I almost forgot to give you this. It was mixed in with our mail that came by post this morning."

He handed her a stained and wrinkled missive that bore foreign markings.

"A letter for me?" she asked in surprise, staring down at it. The writing was squarish, slightly back slanted, and vaguely familiar, stirring in her sudden emotion. Quickly, she thrust the letter into her pocket as though it were burning her fingers. She would wait until George had left to open it.

When he was gone and she was safely upstairs in her chamber, she locked the door to assure that she would not be disturbed. Sitting by the fireplace, she slowly broke the seal. The salutation, "My dearest Heloise," and the signature, "Your Abelard, Antoine," confirmed her suspicion.

Antoine poured out in a torrent of words how, all these years, he had carried, undimmed by time or even marriage, the flaming torch of his love for Diana. He had been in blackest despair after Diana had abandoned him in Geneva. When her mother had written him a few short weeks later that Diana had fallen in love with an English lord on the voyage home and was marrying him, he had been crazed by heartbreak.

Diana gasped, shocked that Mama would have written Antoine such a lie. But Diana remembered well how stubbornly determined her willful mother had been to end the romance, and anger welled up in her at her long-dead parent.

Diana read on. When Lady Landane's letter had reached Antoine, he wrote, he had contemplated suicide. But instead he had succumbed to Simone's pleas that he marry her. After all, what did it matter whom he married when he had lost the one and only woman he would ever love?

His wife, whom he had never been able to love as he had loved Diana, had died some years before in childbed. He had only recently chanced to hear that Diana's mother and grandfather had died and that Diana had never married. He dared to hope that it was because she had never forgotten her Abelard. It was this hope alone that was sustaining him in these dark days when he had once again been forced into exile—this time by the devil dictator Napoleon.

Antoine went on for several additional paragraphs on his love for her in a dazzling array of flowery phrases and metaphors, concluding, "I live now only to see you and to convince you to become my wife."

He wrote that while he could hardly expect her to accept his offer after so long a separation, he begged her to at least meet him so that he could press his suit to her in person. Of course, it would be very dangerous for him. A Frenchman dared not arrive openly in England, where he most likely would be mistaken for a spy. Nevertheless, so great was his love for her, he would happily risk death to sneak into England if she would but agree to meet him at a certain Red Fox Inn on the Sussex coast, where a smuggler's vessel would deposit him. She had only to write him that she would rendezvous with him on the night of February fifteenth, and he would be there.

A rush of emotion swept over Diana as she finished the letter: wistful memories of the love she had had for Antoine, sadness for what might have been, and rage at her mother for writing that lying letter to Antoine. It had been her mother's lie that had been responsible for Antoine's hasty marriage and Diana's misery. Not only did he still remember her; he still loved her and was willing to risk his life to prove it. For a woman who had known too little love in her life, this was heady wine.

But what were her feelings for him? She had put him out of her mind long ago. Much troubled, she folded the letter, remembering Antoine as she had last seen him, so young, so handsome. But that had been nearly eight years before, when she had been a silly girl of sixteen. What would he be like now at thirty? His boyish handsomeness would have faded into a man's face, just as her passion for him had long ago faded into memory. Although the thought of seeing him again excited her, she was much too honest a woman to fool herself into thinking that she still loved him. Too many years had intervened. She would write to him, rejecting his suit as gently as she could.

But first, she thought with dread, she must get through Stratford's unwelcome visit.

CHAPTER 5

On the road from London, the duke of Stratford, in his high-sprung coach with the ducal crest on the door, was contemplating his visit to Greycote with a dread every bit as lively as Diana's. The day was bitter, with a harsh wind shrieking through the trees. The heat had long since faded from the hot bricks that had been provided for the duke's comfort, so that now, despite the fur rugs, he was suffering from cold feet both literally and figuratively.

He groaned aloud as he thought of the interminable boredom that undoubtedly awaited him at Greycote. Not that he regretted leaving London for the country. He was sick to death of balls, routs, and assemblies filled with the frivolous chatter of dandies whose chief interest in life was how well their cravats were tied and of women who cared only for comparing gowns and lovers while their children were left to unloving nannies and incompetent tutors.

Often while in London, the duke would seek relief from his ennui in his sculpture. It would have astonished his peers to learn of this talent, which he kept a carefully hidden secret. His mother had discerned it at an early age and had hired an able teacher for him. Much of his grand tour had been spent in Italy studying the works of masters like Michelangelo.

As the coach rounded a sharp curve, a sudden, sharp gust of wind struck it, and the vehicle swayed alarmingly. Stratford braced himself against the green velvet seat and, thinking of his sculpture, sighed. If only he had more time to devote to it. Still, his pieces had excited some critical attention. He had signed them with the pseudonym Lysipus, a variation of Lysippus, the Greek genius whose busts had so pleased Alexander the Great that he had made him his royal sculptor.

The duke's finest work, the one he most cherished, had been a marble bust of Hamlet. He had never meant to sell it, but three months before, when Charlie had presented him with yet another staggering list of gambling debts, Stratford had been so strapped for ready cash that he had included the Hamlet in a consignment of his work to Debonet, the Bond Street art dealer. Even then, Alexander had stipulated that the Hamlet should not sell for a farthing less than three hundred pounds. He had been certain that no one would pay that for a work, no matter how good, by a little-known sculptor. But, to his shock, sell it had. He had not even been able to learn the identity of the new owner, only that she was a young lady who had taken a great fancy to it.

Someday, Alexander swore to himself, he would find the Hamlet and buy it back, no matter what it cost him, just as he would restore Mistelay to its former splendor.

He stared out the coach window. A hard freeze during the night had scattered glittering diamondlike chips of frost on the ground, the bushes, and the evergreen leaves of the cork oaks. The day seemed to be growing colder, and the skies were shrouded in an ominous gray that promised a storm. He could think of nothing worse than being stranded at Greycote by a heavy snowfall.

His distaste for his visit there had been growing from the moment he had told Landane that he had decided to take a wife and that Miss Landane was "one of a dozen" prospects he was considering.

His lordship had been so thunderstruck at this piece of news that he had been rendered speechless. When finally he had recovered, he had insisted that the duke must visit Greycote to meet his daughter. The duke had agreed only after extracting a promise from Landane that he would tell no one, especially not his daughter, the real purpose of the visit. By the time the duke had managed to escape his lordship, his interest in the daughter had diminished considerably as a result of his exposure to her father.

Stratford wondered whether she was as great a bore as his lordship. He could accept a wife who was not a beauty but not one who was a bore.

Although loveliness was indispensable in a dalliance, other qualities were far more important to him in a wife. As he had told Charlie, he wanted a lively, intelligent woman who would be an entertaining companion to him and a loving mother to his children, a woman who would run his house admirably and see to his comfort.

It would have astounded the ton to know that the haughty duke loved to romp with his nephews and eagerly looked forward to doing the same with his own children. Indeed, the only aspect of his journey to Greycote that still appealed in the slightest to him was the excellent excuse it provided to visit his sister and two young nephews.

By the time the duke reached the posting house, two hours from his destination, where the horses were changed for the final leg, he was sorely tempted to skip Greycote and go directly to his sister's. But this option was suddenly foreclosed by the appearance of Lord Landane on a gray horse.

Alexander stared at Landane in disbelief. Only a complete fool would have ridden horseback such a distance on a day as bitter as this. Indeed, the cold had colored his lordship's face very nearly as scarlet as his riding coat. Although the duke had no taste for Landane's company on the rest of the trip, he was forced to welcome the half-frozen man into his coach.

Since Alexander had first approached Landane, he had made discreet inquiries of him and his daughter. What the duke had learned of his lordship had disgusted him, and what little he had learned of the daughter had been discouraging.

Landane climbed into the coach and settled himself on the green velvet seat beside the duke. Stamping his feet to warm them, Landane immediately launched into a lengthy monologue about the beastliness of the weather. His lordship's habit of talking too much grew more pronounced when he was nervous, and he was apparently exceedingly nervous about the duke's introduction to his daughter.

He earnestly reassured Stratford at least a dozen times that his daughter was quite out of the ordinary. It was true she was no beauty and not much given to conversation, but she was possessed of a myriad of other fine—although vague—qualities.

"She will not bore you with idle chatter, Your Grace," Landane concluded. His nervous fingers played incessantly with the tassels of the coach's green curtains, and he nipped frequently from a brandy flask in his coat pocket.

Instead of reassuring the duke, Landane had thoroughly alarmed him. Good lord, he thought, she must be a fright if even her father can find nothing good to say about her. He was more and more wishing both her and her father to Jericho and wondering how quickly he could escape Greycote. He hoped that at least Landane had invited some diverting guests to dinner that night, but Landane crushed that feeble hope when he said, "You shall have my daughter all to yourself tonight. I was careful to invite no other company."

Stratford scarcely concealed his dismay. The thought of

spending a full night in the company of this bore, who never stopped talking, and his ugly daughter, who apparently never talked at all, was not a prospect he bore with fortitude. "Am I to be your only guest during my stay?"

Landane reddened. "I have invited Lord and Lady Owsley and one of their daughters. They arrive tomorrow morning."

His Grace, who knew full well what a social coup it was to be visited by the duke of Stratford, realized that Landane, to impress his future bride and her parents, had made certain that their visit overlapped his. Stratford wondered with a hint of malicious amusement whether Landane was aware that his young betrothed had desperately tried to snare the duke and had thrown herself at him in a most direct and rather shocking fashion. Stratford, however, had found Isabel Oswley one of the most disagreeable females he had met in recent years.

"Are you acquainted with the Owsleys' daughter, Isabel?" Landane asked.

"Yes."

"A most enchanting creature, isn't she?"

"No," the duke replied bluntly.

Landane looked as though the duke had slapped him. He blustered, then remembering he dared not alienate Stratford, said in a choked voice, "Miss Isabel is betrothed to me."

"Really?" Stratford gave the word just the right twist of incredulity. "But she is so young."

The angry flush on Landane's face told the duke that his lordship was one of those vain, middle-aged men who, despite the image in their mirrors, still stubbornly saw themselves as young and handsome as they had been at twenty.

"I am not an old man," Landane protested hotly.

The duke's grin was decidedly malicious. "But should I marry your daughter, I would have a mother-in-law some years younger than my wife."

This momentarily silenced Landane. In the hope of cutting off further conversation, the duke turned to the window. A male bullfinch with black cap, tail, and wings and rose-red breast, startled by the noise of the passing coach, flew up from his perch on a hawthorn bush. The duke hoped Landane had kept his promise not to tell his daughter the reason for this visit. If she knew the truth, she undoubtedly would shower Alexander with awkward, cloying attention, hanging on his every word and gazing at him with loving, hopeful eyes, all of which he would find exceedingly distasteful.

As the coach turned into the gate of Greycote, it was hardly an inviting sight in the winter bleakness, with its gardens covered by snow and its trees bare of leaves. The duke's foreboding of disaster heightened when he saw the house, a nondescript pile of gray stone, without style or character. Stratford knew the look all too well. It was precisely the sort of house that he was always exceedingly careful to avoid. Inevitably, the furniture would be heavy and clumsy in the Kent style, which he detested, and would be precisely arranged in square, unimaginative blocks. The paintings would be wretched. The guest bedchamber would be damp, dreary, and cramped, without a proper room for his valet Barlow, who was following in the duke's chaise. That would put Barlow, who was more particular about his comfort than even his master was, in a dreadful humor. Furthermore, the chimneys would smoke, the food would be wretched, and the wine worse. The servants would be ill trained, and the daughter of the house would be lacking in all grace and style.

The very gloomiest of Alexander's fears were confirmed when, upon entering the house, he was introduced to Miss Landane.

Although the duke had been forewarned that she was unattractive, he had not expected quite such an antidote. Her hair, pulled back in a severe knot, was drab, and her complexion was such a sickly yellow that he wondered about the state of her liver. Her sullen eyes peered coldly at him from behind a hideous pair of steel-framed spectacles, and he could not imagine why any woman would wear such a singularly unstylish and unbecoming dress.

Suppressing his dismay, he lied, "It is such a pleasure to meet you, Miss Landane." He gave her a winning smile.

She did not seem to notice. "We have met before," she told him coldly.

With some effort, Alexander concealed his surprise. He said smoothly, "It must have been a long time ago, I should surely have remembered."

"Years ago, but that does not signify. You had already forgotten me when I saw you the next night."

He bit back a cruel comment on what a forgettable creature she was and changed the subject. "It was very kind of you to permit me to enjoy your hospitality on such short notice." He gave her his most dazzling smile, the one guaranteed to bring any female to her knees.

Miss Landane appeared not the slightest affected.

Alexander could not detect the slightest spark of the spirit and humor that he had hoped to find in her. His mind was already firmly made up: There was no way on earth that he would offer for such a creature no matter how large her fortune. Even his great love for Mistelay could not bring him to that. He longed to leave Greycote immediately, but he would have to spend at least the night.

"I understand that you will be with us, Your Grace, until the day after tomorrow." Miss Landane's thin, monotonous voice held no hint of welcome.

Stratford seized the opportunity to extradite himself quickly from the disastrous visit. "I am afraid only until tomorrow morning."

"What?" The distress in Landane's voice was unmistakable. "You must stay at least until the Owsleys arrive." His lordship glared at his daughter, and his voice rose in whining desperation. "Alex, you must—"

This unwarranted familiarity was too much for Alexander's already-strained temper. "My name is Alexander," he snapped. "Now, if I may be shown to my room."

To his enormous surprise, he found that instead of a cramped bedchamber he had been allocated a spacious apartment that included sitting and dressing rooms. All was immaculate, the artfully arranged furniture was French, and the upholstery and hangings were of a cheerful blue-and-white chintz. A newly laid fire crackled in the fireplace, which did not smoke in the slightest. The water in the ewer was hot. A handsome vase of yellow roses sat on a table, and on another decanters of brandy and port rested on a small silver tray. The suite exuded a cheerful comfort.

Alexander was far more favorably impressed by the house than by its mistress. He was particularly struck by the paintings. Instead of the dreadful family portraits by talentless artists that were so often found in small country houses, the walls were hung with excellent landscapes.

Stratford was particularly intrigued by a landscape in his bedchamber in which an unsettled lavender sky seemed to reflect its disturbance on the trees, the land, and the lake beneath it. The whole was bathed in a strange and luminous light, and he was struck by the artist's remarkable and original perception of it. The painting was signed with dramatic initials so intertwined that he could not make out their separate identity.

He had noticed another landscape hanging in the hall near the door to his apartment that had also caught his interest. Picking up a bronze chamberstick, he lit the candle from the fire and headed for the hall to examine the painting more closely. But as his hand turned the knob of his door, he heard a noise in the hall. Cautiously, he opened the door only a tiny crack and saw Landane weaving down the hallway. His lordship apparently had continued making indentures in the brandy after Alexander had come upstairs. From the evil look on his lordship's face, the duke concluded Landane was not a pleasant drunk.

His lordship lurched against a door across the hall from the duke's and unceremoniously burst through it with such violence that it cracked against the wall and bounced forward again.

The duke caught a glimpse of Miss Landane's startled face and heard her father growl, "You wretched vixen, I might have known you would ruin everything."

Stratford heard her exclaim, "What are you talking about?" Then the door slammed shut, preventing further eavesdropping.

The duke was certain that Landane, in his drunken temper, was telling his daughter of Alexander's interest in her, and he could cheerfully have strangled the besotted fool. Her awareness that she was being looked over by the duke would only exacerbate what already promised to be a dreadful dinner. She would no doubt fawn over him in an attempt to win his favor, and the prospect filled him with dread. Yet he could not help feeling sorry for the poor, drab creature. His exposure to her pleasant household had left the duke feeling somewhat more kindly disposed toward her.

But his softened feelings hardened instantly when she entered the dining parlor that evening. She had changed into a gown, if that's what it could be called, that quite stunned the duke. It was a coatlike affair of black silk, pleated at the shoulders and falling in voluminous folds, like a giant tent, to the floor. It looked more like a domino one would wear to a masquerade than a gown for dinner. The costume was so bizarre that Alexander wondered whether she was an eccentric.

Nor was the rest of her appearance any more pleasing. Her hair was still pulled back severely into a knot in back, which emphasized her owllike face, dominated by the thick, steel-rimmed glasses. Her complexion seemed even sallower than it had that afternoon, and he could swear the circles beneath her eyes were darker.

Seeing the hard, determined look in her bespectacled eyes, Stratford thought, God, I am in for it now. But to his surprise, instead of trying desperately to win his interest by an effusive display, she seemed to be struck dumb.

Dinner was served at precisely the appointed hour. The table was beautifully laid with crystal and Meissen china. More roses brightened the dining parlor. The food was excellent and well served. The wines were of a quality Stratford would have found acceptable in his own cellar and superbly matched to the various courses. It was a remarkable culinary feat for a small country kitchen.

Unfortunately, the company fell far short of matching the caliber of the food. At first, Landane seemed determined to make up for his daughter's silence by talking with the rambling loquaciousness of a man more than a little foxed. After his lordship had discoursed at considerable, if disjointed, length upon the merits of port wine, the duke could not resist saying coldly, "I prefer Madeira."

But as his lordship resorted frequently to his wineglass, his conversation became fuzzier and more infrequent until he lapsed into a sort of semistupor. The meal proceeded in uncomfortable silence. Since Miss Landane made no attempt at conversation, the duke felt that out of politeness he must try. Nodding toward the flowers, he said, "I am amazed to find such beautiful roses here at this time of year."

The hard eyes behind the glasses softened slightly. "Flowers are my great weakness. I love them, and I have a hothouse in which I grow them."

Alexander wondered what her eyes would look like

unconcealed by the thick round lens. "Must you always wear your eyeglasses?" he asked.

"I am quite blind without them," she assured him, staring down at her plate.

"You have a very comfortable and attractive home here," Alexander observed. His compliment was sincere, but he doubted that she had been responsible for it, done as it was with an artist's eye for color, balance, and design.

"Thank you," she said coolly. "Father was quite distressed with me when I redid it like this. He finds it too light and informal."

Alexander regarded her questioningly, mystified by how a woman whose home showed so much style and taste could exhibit none in her own dress and appearance. Furthermore, he found her habit of fixing her gaze sullenly downward even when she addressed him directly most disconcerting. He wondered whether she was excessively shy or merely stupid.

Silence settled in again. Alexander's desultory attempts to draw Miss Landane into new topics of conversation failed. Never had he met a hostess who took such good care of her guest's physical comfort but made no effort to put him at his ease personally.

Alexander was relieved on one score, however. Her father most certainly could not have told her the reason for his visit, for she was making no effort whatsoever to fix his interest. Indeed, her sullen silence was guaranteed to drive him away.

Alexander resigned himself to an interminable evening in the company of this farouche girl and her drunken father. But as dessert was served, Miss Landane broke the silence to inform him, "I have invited our neighbors, Squire Whorton and his son, after dinner. I think Your Grace may find them pleasant company."

Her words roused her father from his torpor. "You have

done what? How dare you invite guests without consulting me?"

"I was persuaded the duke would enjoy meeting our neighbors, and you rode out before I could ask you this morning."

The duke was thankful for any relief from the two Landanes, but he hoped that Whorton would not be one of those squires who smelled of their horses and whose conversation was as coarse as their persons.

"If you must invite guests, why not Squire Stevens?" Landane's voice was slurred with alcohol. "He has a hunter I have been trying to bargain him out of."

"Squire Stevens is a crude oaf who stinks of his stables and can talk of nothing but wine, wenches, and horses," Miss Landane replied calmly. "I am persuaded that even if his conversation failed to disgust His Grace, his smell most certainly would."

Stratford regarded Miss Landane with new interest. She was not quite the idiot he had thought her.

CHAPTER 6

The Whortons, father and son, bought with them a surprise for Diana. She let out a shriek of startled delight as she saw Elizabeth Hill precede her father and brother into Greycote. The eyes behind the ugly spectacles flashed with delight.

"Eliza, when did you arrive?" Diana cried as she hugged

her friend. "George, the wretch, didn't say a word to me about your coming when he was here this morning."

"I surprised them," Mrs. Hill replied. "Edward had to go to London, and I persuaded him to take me as far as Papa's so that the children and I might visit."

"The girls are with you?" Diana's face flushed with excitement and delight. "I cannot wait to see them. Why didn't you bring them tonight?"

Mrs. Hill laughed. "Diana, you are as bad as my daughters. They are both sulking at Papa's, asking the very same thing. All they talked of on the journey today was seeing you." She gave Diana a fond smile and said teasingly, "I am afraid I am only a poor second in their affections behind you."

"Nonsense," Diana said briskly, "but I do so want to see them. Promise me that you will bring them to me in the morning as soon as they are up."

"Six A.M. is rather an early hour to call," George interposed.

"I shall not mind in the least," Diana retorted. "I am an early riser."

The duke was intrigued by the change that Mrs. Hill's arrival had wrought in Miss Landane. Not only was it by far the most animation that he had seen that dull, sullen lump exhibit since his arrival, but even her thin, monotonous voice had acquired timbre and color.

"Where is Mrs. Cottam?" Eliza asked.

"I fear the duke's visit was too much for her," Diana replied in a low voice. "She worked herself into such a state of nerves that she had to take to her bed before he even arrived."

Alexander, whose sharp gray eyes missed little, noted that George had been studying Miss Landane with a peculiar glint in his eye during her conversation with his sister. As Landane was introducing the duke to Mrs. Hill, he overheard George ask bluntly, "Diana, where the devil did you get that awful gown—if that's what it is?"

Since this was the very question Alexander himself had longed to ask, he strained to hear her reply.

She smiled innocently. "Don't you like it?"

"It is positively the ugliest thing I have ever seen."

George instantly won Alexander's liking. He preferred honest men who did not mince words. A smile tugged at his lips as he waited for the storm of reproach that would surely come from Miss Landane.

"Do you really think so?" she asked, unmistakable delight in her voice.

George's voice dropped to a whisper. Alexander strained his ears, but the squire's booming voice beside him drowned out all else. It was just as well for the duke's self-esteem that he could not hear.

"What game are you up to now, Diana?" George whispered. "Are you deliberately trying to disgust His Arrogance with your appearance?"

She nodded. "Even his famous charm very nearly fled when he saw me. You would have been much amused, George."

"His Arrogance will make you the laughingstock of London," George warned.

"Better than his wife."

George glanced at the elegant, wickedly handsome duke, the picture of urbane sophistication in his coat of blue velour with white appliqué trim on the cuffs and pockets and his white satin waistcoat with silver floss. George burst out laughing. "You featherhead, Diana. I have never known you to entertain unwarranted conceit of yourself before, but the idea of His Arrogance making you an offer is ridiculous."

"I am sparing no effort to make certain he agrees with you," she replied cordially, a determined gleam in her eyes.

Alexander, unable to hear any of this exchange, wondered what had prompted George's laughter. The duke discovered to his great relief that Squire Whorton was both intelligent and plainspoken. He had a forthrightness coupled with a vast store of common sense that pleased Alexander far more than the artificial conversation of a London dandy ever would have. The two men were soon deep in a discussion of the disastrous crop failures of the previous two years that, coupled with the war against Napoleon and the Corsican's continental blockade, had left the British economy in a sad state.

"This is one of the cruelest winters I have seen here in twenty years," the squire said. "If it is a harbinger of what is to come, it will be another disastrous year. Mark my word, Your Grace; another season of ruined crops and the consequences will be catastrophic. Already many poor tenants cannot pay their rents, cannot even afford food for their families. There will be rebellions. Mark my word. There will—"

He broke off as his son joined them. "George, I was telling the duke about the plight of the poor tenants." The squire turned his steady gaze back upon the duke. "They are being driven out of their homes by rich landowners because they cannot pay their rents. You rich aristocrats give no thought to anything but your own pleasures. You complain bitterly of the increases in your taxes, but while they are onerous, they are not fatal. But mark my word. Your selfish shortsightedness is not only inhumane; it is bad politics."

George looked thoroughly alarmed at his father's bluntness. He obviously expected the squire's impertinence to draw a severe setdown from the haughty duke, and he said hastily, "Pa, I don't expect His Grace came here to have you lecture him on the responsibilities of the aristocracy."

"Your father is right," Alexander replied calmly. "In some counties people are starving already. It is shameful."

The three men were soon discussing John Locke's theories on the natural right to property. George, who had inherited his sire's common sense and candor, was another pleasant surprise for Alexander, who was most grateful to Miss Landane for having invited them.

His lordship remained in his large armchair, sunk in a morose stupor. He exhibited no interest in his guests but contented himself with making deep indentures in the decanter of brandy on the table beside his chair.

"I must apologize for our host," the squire said finally. "I assure you his wretched manners are not the usual custom here. He's of fine blood, but you'd never know it." Pity crept into the squire's voice. "To think that once he was the handsomest young man for twenty leagues hereabout. Never had good bottom, though."

"Pa blames his marriage," George put in. "Says it was the ruination of both him and his lady."

"I gather it was not a love match," Alexander said.

The squire shook his head. "No. She was madly in love with a most ineligible young officer from the colonies and eloped to Gretna Green with him. Her father, old John Wakely, would have none of such a match. He caught them before they could be wed and dragged her back to London. He was obliged to find her a suitable husband who would be willing to overlook the scandal."

Alexander grinned. "And Landane was happy to do so for a price."

"I don't believe he did it only for the money, although his lady was convinced that was his sole reason. She never let off harping at him that he was a fortune hunter who had married her only for her father's fortune. But in truth she was quite a belle, and he had a tendre for her. He was still very handsome then and so vain that I think he believed she would be overjoyed and eternally grateful to have him as a husband after her elopement had cast such a cloud over her reputation.''

"But she was not?" The duke flicked a minuscule piece of lint from his impeccable coat.

"She hated him for it," the squire said bluntly. "She thought that if he had not stepped in and agreed to marry her, her father eventually would have been forced to accept her lover. It was a marriage made in hell. A stubborn, contemptuous wife and a vain weakling of a husband. Landane tried to cow her, but she was far too spirited, and he was far too weak. He only succeeded in making her despise him the more. Finally, he ordered her here to Greycote until she should agree to be the dutiful, loving wife he wanted. Of course, she never did. And he turned to drink for solace. As the years have gone by, he has become steadily more dissipated.''

"Poor Diana," George said.

"Aye, she's a wonderful lass," his father said. "Has her mother's good points without the bad.''

This accolade surprised Alexander, and he turned to study his hostess. She was deeply engrossed in a conversation with Mrs. Hill. Her sullenness had vanished. Her laugh, as melodious as chimes, floated across the room. It seemed quite out of keeping with the thin, monotonous voice he had heard during dinner.

George, as though drawn by her laugh, moved to join her and his sister. Intrigued, Alexander followed, but Miss Landane immediately fell silent and slipped away, leaving him with George and Mrs. Hill.

Later, seeing George and Miss Landane talking together, Alexander moved toward them and made out that they were discussing a book.

"I suppose you are talking about Mrs. Radcliffe's latest masterpiece." He was unable to keep a hint of sarcasm from his voice.

"I am sorry to disappoint you, Your Grace," Miss Landane replied coldly, "but I am not an admirer of hers. We were discussing Alexander Pope's 'Imitations of Horace.' "

"Pope?" he repeated, taken aback.

"Perhaps you have heard of him?" she asked innocently.

"Of course, I—" He broke off, realizing that she was hoaxing him, and said, "I would not have thought he would appeal to you."

"Why not?" Her voice was sharp.

"It is not the usual romantic fare that young ladies read."

"Your Grace, I am not the usual young lady, and I am not the least romantic." She turned abruptly and walked away, leaving Alexander alone with George.

Alexander, seeing the amused affection in George's eyes as he watched her retreat, was suddenly suspicious. "You seem very fond of Miss Landane."

The young man nodded. "I consider her as much my sister as Eliza. The three of us grew up together."

Alexander smiled. "I thought perhaps your feelings might be more than merely brotherly."

"It's a fact that she's the only girl I know whom I could imagine being shackled to." George's frank brown eyes met Alexander's gray ones squarely. "I told her that once, but she just laughed at me. She said we were so much brother and sister that it would be incestuous."

"You would want to marry her?" The disbelief in Alexander's voice brought an angry flush to George's cheeks. "There must be more to her than meets the eye."

"To the contrary, Your Grace, I would say there is rather less to her," George replied tartly.

"What do you mean?

"You disappoint me, Your Grace. You are not so acute as your reputation makes you out to be." George turned on his heel and walked away.

Landane roused from his stupor and ordered Diana to entertain them with a song on her harp. She tried to refuse, but he became so surly that she acquiesced to avoid a scene.

"Her talent will delight Your Grace," her father loudly assured Alexander. "I've no ear myself, but I know talent like hers when I hear it."

She cast her father a baleful look as she made her way reluctantly to the harp.

Astonished rather than delighted more accurately described the duke's reaction to what he readily admitted was a unique musical performance. Never in his life had he heard anything quite like it, and he fervently hoped he never would again. Her voice and harp frequently moved in opposite directions on the scale. The cadenzas were showy in a way no composer ever intended. Alexander found her voice equally stunning. Harsh and brassy, it had the ear-jarring habit of sliding up or down the scale toward the right note and generally missing it.

Alexander looked around at his fellow sufferers. Mrs. Hill and her father seemed stupefied. Landane, who was rapidly downing yet another glass of brandy, looked puzzled. Only George was enjoying the performance hugely. In fact, he was shaking with laughter. Finally, when it appeared he no longer could contain himself, he fled from the room.

When Miss Landane concluded, her listeners could not force themselves to ask for an encore.

As she rose from the harp, Landane staggered up to the duke and seized his arm. "I told you my daughter was quite out of the ordinary." His lordship's breath was heavy with brandy, and his voice was tinged with desperation. "She would make you a fine wife." Even Landane, drunk as he was, had difficulty getting out this forlorn lie.

Alexander fixed him with his coldest, most disdainful

stare. "Nothing on earth could persuade me to marry your daughter."

"She is immensely rich."

"Not rich enough," the duke snapped. "The entire contents of the British treasury would not be sufficient to persuade me to marry that farouche creature."

Alexander pulled his arm free. Turning, he discovered that George, having recovered his composure, had returned and had been directly behind him. Although the young man was carefully studying a handsome landscape of the Devon coast signed with the same intertwining initials as the work in the duke's bedchamber, he most certainly must have overheard the exchange between Landane and Alexander. George turned and sauntered over to Miss Landane and his sister.

Alexander drew in his breath sharply as George began telling the two women something. Surely the young man could not be repeating what Alexander had just said to Landane about not marrying his daughter. A look of pure delight flashed across Miss Landane's sallow face, and the duke was much relieved. Obviously, George had not betrayed the conversation that he had just overheard.

The Whorton party departed a few minutes later. Before Alexander could escape upstairs, Landane cornered him and insisted his reluctant guest share a glass of wine with him before retiring.

To Alexander's acute distress, Landane poured out his version of his unhappy marriage along with the wine.

"Should've been grateful to me for marrying her after she ran off with 'er lover." The liquor had thickened and slurred his speech. " 'Stead, the chit cursed me, saying I'd've married a cow if its dowry'd been large enough. That's the thanks I got. A terrible life it was, married to that shrew." Landane flung his hand out drunkenly, knocking over his nearly empty glass. What was left of its contents dripped over the table edge and onto his leg, but he did not notice. "Turned my only child against me, too."

He slumped down in his chair in a stupor. Alexander quickly escaped upstairs to his bedchamber, where he found his valet awaiting him.

As Barlow helped his master out of his velour coat, he said, "Best-run house I've been in since Your Grace's mama presided at Mistelay."

Alexander regarded his usual laconic valet with surprise, for he was more difficult than even his master to please.

After Barlow left him, Alexander went to the table that held the decanters and was surprised to find that a third—of Madeira—had been added to the silver tray. He remembered his remark at dinner about preferring Madeira.

Yes, a very well run house. If only its mistress were not so utterly lacking in wit and charm.

CHAPTER 7

The bracket clock in the guest bedchamber read ten before eight, which for the duke was an exceedingly early hour to awaken. It would be at least two hours before breakfast was served and he would be able to make his escape from Greycote. He rose and went to the window. Opening the draperies, he found the windowpanes so heavily encrusted with frost that he could scarcely see the gray world beyond. It was a most dismal day, and it contrasted sharply with the pleasant comfort of his room.

The house was as quiet as a tomb. Undoubtedly, he was the first to rise. It would be an opportune time to slip down to the drawing room with his quizzing glass and study more closely a painting of the royal crescent at Bath hanging there. He had admired it the night before, but he had not had a chance to examine it closely. He had noticed, however, that it bore the same intertwining artists's initials as several other paintings in the house that he particularly liked.

Confident that no one would be about at such an early hour, the duke put on a brocade dressing gown and went downstairs. As he neared the drawing room, he heard the soft limpid tones of the harp, stroked by loving fingers that possessed far greater talent than Miss Landane's had the previous night. He paused and listened in appreciation to a dazzling cadenza full of demanding tricks performed with the skill of a virtuoso.

Not wanting to interrupt this concert, he bypassed the drawing room and slipped quietly into the small sitting room that adjoined it. The door between the two rooms was open. Alexander could scarcely believe his eyes when he saw that it was Miss Landane, sitting with her back to him, at the harp. He sank down in a chair, enchanted by the silvery chords that rippled from her fingers.

A moment later her voice softly joined the harp. It had none of the harshness or sliding uncertainty of the previous night; it was as sweet and pure and true as the harp, never faltering on even the most difficult notes. He sat mesmerized in his chair until she finished.

She rose from the harp and walked to the hall door, still unaware that he was watching her. She wore the same ugly gray dress that she had had on the previous day when he had arrived. She did have an excellent figure, slender and full-breasted, and the good sense not to contort it with corsets and stays. Alexander had a sculptor's appreciation of the human form, and he hated to see women torture their lovely bodies into unnatural lines.

Diana disappeared into the hall. He remained in his seat, mulling over the enormous difference between her performance the night before and that morning.

A portrait of the late Lady Landane as a young girl hung above the fireplace. Alexander got up and went over to study it more closely. She had been a lovely woman. Her eyes sparkled with mischief, her complexion was fine, and her hair was the color of spun gold. And—only a sculptor like him might have noticed—she had exquisite bone structure: high, prominent cheekbones, a slightly upturned nose, and a strong chin.

A loud knock sounded at the front door, and he heard Miss Landane's quick step in the hall. The door opened, and he heard Mrs. Hill saying, "We came so early because I fear a terrible storm is on the way and we will not be able to make it later."

The duke stepped back in the shadows of the sitting room so that he could observe the scene in the hall without its participants being aware of his presence. Mrs. Hill was accompanied by her daughters, who, Alexander had learned the night before, were two and four years old. It was obvious from the delighted squeals of the pair and from the way they hurled themselves into Diana's arms that she was a great favorite of theirs. It was obvious, too, from the strength of the hug that Diana gave them and the doting sparkle in her eyes that she loved them.

Watching her caught in the children's embrace, Alexander suddenly realized that she was not wearing her dreadful spectacles. How lovely her dancing blue eyes were without them. And how like her mother's was her bone structure: the same high, prominent cheekbones, delightful nose, strong chin. Why, then, was she so unattractive? One answer was that dreadful sallow complexion that made her look as though she were suffering from an advanced case of the jaundice; a second was the severe hairstyle that he had never before seen on a woman under sixty; third, those dreadful eyeglasses; and finally, her sullen silence.

Diana extracted herself from the girls' embraces. The elder girl, her face troubled, stared up at her. "Auntie Diana, is you sick?"

"No. What makes you think so, Betsy?"

"You look strange—your skin and hair's not like it used to be."

"You do look dreadful, Diana," their mother said.

Diana laughed. "I know. Isn't it wonderful?" She grabbed each girl's hand and led them toward a room at the back of the house. "Come, I have made each of you a book."

The girls squealed with delight.

Alexander waited a full minute after the little party had disappeared before he left the sitting room and made his way unnoticed upstairs. He thought of George's remark that there was rather less to Miss Landane than met the eye. Alexander was becoming more and more intrigued by her.

So preoccupied was he with his thoughts that he did not notice until he was dressed that he had left his quizzing glass downstairs. He had laid it on a table in the sitting room while he had listened to Miss Landane's lovely performance.

Cursing his forgetfulness, he went back downstairs to retrieve his glass. He got as far as the sitting-room door when his leg was attacked by a wee creature. Looking down, he discovered Mrs. Hill's younger daughter, a plump pretty child with wispy brown hair that curled about her face. Her great brown eyes regarded him impishly.

When she saw the surprise in his eyes, she laughed gleefully. "I's a new book." She still clung to his leg, both fat little arms wrapped tightly around it.

He grinned down at her. "Do you, now? I'll wager your Auntie Diana made it for you."

She nodded.

"What's your name?"

She turned coquettish. "Guess!" She giggled.

"Pumpkin."

Her brown eyes grew round with surprise. "No," she said reproachfully.

"I like Pumpkin. I am renaming you Pumpkin."

She looked at him uncertainly, then said gravely, "I's Amy."

"I'm Alexander."

The child's inexperienced tongue stumbled over the several syllables of his name: "'l's'an'er."

The duke laughed. "Call me Alex. It's easier."

" 'lex," she assayed.

"That's close." He reached down to disengage the plump arms from his leg.

"Are you visiting A'tie D'ana?" she asked as he separated her arms gently.

"Sort of." The duke dropped to his knee so that he might talk to the little girl without towering over her.

"I love A'tie D'ana," she confided. "She's my favoritest person."

CHAPTER 8

"I cannot tell you, Eliza, how shocked and wretched I was when father told me before dinner last night that Stratford was thinking of offering for me." Diana's voice was choked with emotion as she sat with Mrs. Hill on the sofa by the fireplace in the room at the back of the house that was Diana's private retreat.

More than any other room it reflected Diana's own personality. Comfortable chairs and the sofa were covered in a colorful chintz with large roses against a white background. Her favorite paintings and sculpture, the latter a recently acquired bust of Hamlet, were there. So was the Meissen porcelain of a lady with a lapdog nestled on her vast skirt that had been her mother's favorite.

A large mullioned window looked out on the gardens, now buried beneath a crusted layer of snow bespeckled with soot. The sight was dreary now, with only a few white snowdrops hardy enough to defy the winter cold in bloom. But in summer, when the gardens were alive with colorful masses of flowers, the view was stunning. It was in this room that Diana worked on her household accounts, drew up her menus, and sometimes even labored on her paintings. The light was often better there than in the tiny room on the north side of the house that was her studio.

"But why should you be so distressed, Diana?" Eliza's brown eyes regarded Diana questioningly. "The duke's excessively handsome and charming. He is quite the most eligible catch. Hundreds of girls would be thrilled at the prospect of an offer from him."

"They are welcome to him!"

Eliza gave Diana a skeptical smile. "Aren't you just a

little bit flattered that the elusive duke of Stratford thought of offering for you?''

"If he had been interested in me and not just my fortune, I might have been.''

"Why should the duke be after your fortune? He has estates of his own.''

Diana shrugged. "He is notorious for squandering vast sums on his lights of love. Perhaps he has finally succeeded in emptying even his rich purse on his convenients and finds he must now replenish it.''

Eliza's eyes were troubled, and she stared into the slowly dying fire. "Diana, I know in what terror you hold fortune hunters. Your mother was fanatical in her warnings to you. But I fear you have taken them so to heart that you regard every man who looks at you as a fortune hunter.''

"Why else would the duke think of offering for me?'' Diana jumped up from her chair in agitation and stirred the fire into renewed life with a poker. "He has not seen me in years and did not even remember ever meeting me. He was hardly drawn by my reputation for beauty and charm.''

"You are amply endowed with both.''

"But he knows naught of that.''

"Nor of your musical talent, either, after that singular concert you gave last night,'' Eliza said dryly.

Diana giggled as she resumed her seat beside her friend. "But I thought I was magnificent. It is very difficult indeed to be as bad as that. But it worked. The look on Stratford's face was delicious. It was right after my sterling performance that Stratford told father he would not marry me if my fortune were as large as the British treasury.''

Eliza laid her hand softly on Diana's arm. "It seems to me that proves he is not a fortune hunter.''

"It seems to me that it proves nothing of the sort.''

"Nonsense,'' Eliza said briskly. "Of course he would expect his bride to be well fixed, just as he would expect her to be of excellent character and breeding. A man of his distinguished lineage and title could no more marry a penniless waif than he could wed one of the muslin company, not because he's a fortune hunter but because he knows what is due his family. A great many papas would be delighted to give a large dowry to make their daughters Stratford's duchess, and both they and their offspring would be well satisfied with the bargain.''

"I want no part of such a bargain nor of the duke.''

Eliza toyed with the scarf end of her cream satin tippet. "I do not understand why you find him so objectionable. Papa liked him exceedingly, and you know Papa is not easily fooled by manners when character is deficient. Even George was pleasantly surprised and allowed as we were riding home that 'His Arrogance' was not as bad as his reputation made him out. George thinks he has been maligned.''

"It would be impossible to malign Stratford.'' Diana gazed angrily out the mullioned window. It had begun to snow, and the wind was rising, ruffling the branches of the pines. "I cannot imagine anything worse than being married to that arrogant, conceited rake, who would no doubt throw my money away on his mistresses while I was left alone, ignored and humiliated.'' She shuddered at the thought of what life with the duke would be like.

"I think you are too harsh on the duke, Diana. I do not think he would treat his wife that way. And just think. You would have children of your own. You adore children so.''

"What a dreadful father Stratford would make,'' Diana cried. The anger in her blue eyes was undisguised by her spectacles, which she had left upstairs. "He is certain to detest children, and they would be as neglected as his wife.''

"Speaking of children,'' Eliza said, looking about the room, "where has Amy gone? She was here just a minute ago.''

Diana looked about the room. Betsy, the four-year-old, was sitting quietly on the rug, studying the book that Diana had made for her, but Amy was nowhere in sight. "She must have wandered into the hall," Diana said, getting up to help search for the child.

At the door to the hall, Diana stopped dead in astonishment at the sight of Amy deep in a solemn conversation with the duke of Stratford. Had Diana not seen the scene with her own eyes, she would never have believed that Stratford would so lower his consequence as to take the slightest notice of the toddler.

"Amy, come here," her shocked mother ordered.

The duke stood up and started to take a step back, but Amy seized his leg and clutched it tenaciously in her fat little arms so that he was trapped in place. Diana's eyes sparkled, and her shoulders shook silently with laughter at the sight.

Stratford was, as always, impeccably clad. His coat was of green superfine, his cravat tied with a perfection that Beau Brummel would have envied, and his fine ruffled shirt imported from Holland.

"Good morning, ladies," he said pleasantly. If His Grace felt any loss of dignity at being encumbered by the chubby anchor that clung to his leg, he gave no sign of it.

"Amy, let go of the duke," her mother said in consternation.

But Amy only clung the more firmly. "He says he'll read me the book that A'tie D'ana made for me, won't you, 'lex?" She looked up pleadingly at the figure that now towered above her.

"Amy," Diana said firmly, remembering the reprimand the duke had given her father the previous night for daring to call him Alex, "his name is Alexander."

"No," Amy replied with equal firmness. "His name's 'lex. He told me so."

Diana was at a loss to know what to do. She could hardly reach down and forcibly free the duke's leg from Amy's grasp. "I am so sorry, Your Grace."

The duke laughed. Diana was startled by how warm his gray eyes could be.

"Why should you be?" he asked pleasantly. "Amy and I have been having a delightful little talk." Bending down, he disengaged her arms and swooped her up in his arms. "Up you go, Pumpkin," he said, boosting her high over his head. "See how tall you are now!"

Amy shrieked with glee at her sudden elevation in the world.

The duke sat Amy on his shoulders. Her pudgy little hands first buried themselves in his jet black hair, ruffling the neatly brushed locks, then slipped down to clutch the perfectly tied folds of his snowy white cravat. Her fat little legs dangled carelessly against his elegant coat.

"Your Grace," Eliza said in horror, "I fear she is ruining your clothes."

He dismissed her concern with a smile. "It's of no consequence," he said with such affability that Eliza and Diana exchanged astonished glances. "I have others with me." He started toward the room at the back of the house from which the two women had emerged. Diana was seized by a sudden, inexplicable reluctance to permit him to see her private sanctum. Quickly, she guided him toward the drawing room, saying, "We shall be more comfortable here."

From her perch on Alexander's shoulders, Amy surveyed the drawing room and announced, "I likes your room better, A'tie D'ana."

Betsy appeared in the doorway, carrying both books that Diana had made for her and her sister.

Amy loosened her grip on the duke's cravat, and he put her gently down on her feet. She reached for her book. "'lex is going to read it to me, aren't you, 'lex?"

"Of course I am, Pumpkin," the duke said.

Diana turned scarlet with embarrassment at the thought of the sophisticated duke's mocking eyes perusing the book she had made. She snatched it from Betsy's hand and said, "I will read it to you, Amy."

"No," Amy insisted. "I wants 'lex to."

The duke, his gray eyes much amused, held out his hand to Diana. "Please give me the book, since it is quite impossible for you to read it to her."

"What do you mean?" Diana demanded.

"You are not wearing your eyeglasses." He grinned mockingly. "And you have assured me, you will remember, that you are quite blind without them."

Diana gasped, and her free hand flew up involuntarily to her temples. She felt rather as if she had just been checkmated in a game of chess with the duke. She flushed crimson as she stared into his penetrating gray eyes. He gently took the book from her hand and settled himself on a sofa.

Amy immediately scrambled up and into his lap.

"Amy," her mother pleaded, "get off the duke's lap."

But the little girl shook her brown curls defiantly. Stratford only smiled at her and opened the book.

Diana and Eliza stared in fascination as the formidable duke read in an animated voice the fanciful tale of a dog and cat who once had been enemies but who became fast, if improbable, friends. Diana had illustrated the book with drawings of a terrier and a calico cat.

Outside, the wind had picked up strength and was whistling through the pines and the barren branches of the elm trees. The snow was falling hard now, biting, wind-whipped little flakes, but Diana did not notice in her embarrassment as she listened to the duke and Amy solemnly discuss the story she had written. Her cheeks burned bright with mortification. Stratford glanced up and, seeing her expression, asked, "Whatever is the matter, Miss Landane?"

"Your Grace," she replied in a small, miserable voice, "I made that poor book for Amy, not for your contemptuous amusement."

"Contemptuous? But my dear Miss Landane, you do both yourself and me an injustice. Your book is so charming I should like to commission you to do one for my nephews."

"You are hoaxing me, Your Grace."

"I am not. Why should you think that?"

Diana did not answer him, and he continued to regard her with veiled gray eyes that gave no clue to his thoughts.

To break the uncomfortable silence, Eliza said, "You should see the girls' nursery. When Diana visited us last summer, she decorated the walls with wonderfully whimsical characters. Every child in the neighborhood begs to play there."

She broke off at the sudden appearance of her brother in the doorway. "George, why are you here?"

"Pa sent me. We are in for a fierce storm. It's already starting, and he wanted me to make certain that you and the girls get back safely to Beaconstone."

As if in confirmation of his words, the shoulders of George's gray redingote already were encrusted with white. Looking out the window, Diana saw that the snow was falling so hard now that even the trees were obscured.

"Hurry and get the girls ready," George told his sister. "I fear the road will soon be blocked by drifts the way the wind is blowing."

George's words moved the duke to action, too. As Eliza and Diana bundled the two little girls into their coats and woolens, he gave orders for his team to be harnessed post-haste and for his luggage to be brought down.

"I want to stay with 'lex and D'ana." Amy pouted, her lower lip trembling.

"But I must go, too, Pumpkin," the duke told her, patting her cheek. "Otherwise, the storm may strand me here for several days."

Diana offered a silent prayer that this would not happen.

When the girls were ready to leave, Diana knelt down to receive their farewell hugs and kisses.

Their mother, who was standing beside the duke, remarked in an undertone, "Diana has a great talent with children. My girls adore her."

"Perhaps she will have many of her own," he replied carelessly.

Eliza's face clouded. "She would be such a wonderful mother, but she insists she will never marry."

"That would make having children, if not difficult, at least unconventional," he said dryly. "Why is she so opposed to marriage?"

"I blame it on her mother. She instilled such a vivid terror in Diana of unscrupulous men who would seek her merely for her fortune."

The duke's arched right eyebrow rose. "Miss Landane runs a superlative house," he remarked casually.

Eliza smiled. "Yes, doesn't she? And it is all the more astonishing when one considers the minuscule budget her father permits her."

"Clutch-fisted, is he?" the duke asked.

"Disgracefully so," Eliza agreed. "If it were not for Diana, this house would cost him twice as much with half the result."

Amy came up to the duke. "I want to kiss you 'bye, 'lex."

"No, Amy," her horrified mother said sharply.

But Alexander dropped to his knee. "When a lady as charming as this offers me a kiss, I am honored." He inclined his head toward the little girl so that she could plant a loud, wet smack upon his cheek. Then, with her clutching his forefinger in her tiny, fat fist, he rose and walked her to the door.

Diana watched the duke's genial behavior with amazement so intense it bordered on disbelief. She was seeing a totally unexpected side of Stratford.

As Squire Whorton's carriage pulled away from Greycote, Amy was still waving a vigorous farewell to Alexander.

After the carriage disappeared from sight, Diana said, "You have made yet another conquest, Your Grace."

He grinned. "I am not certain which of us was the conquered."

Despite the duke's desire for haste, more than a half hour elapsed before his equipment was ready and his luggage stowed away.

The wind had risen to an alarming velocity, driving the snow like bits of shrapnel and piling it into high drifts. Diana watched Stratford climb into his coach with considerable misgivings at his starting out in such weather, but she had no desire to dissuade him from departing. She could think of nothing more dreadful than to have him snowbound at Greycote for so much as an hour.

When he was gone, she gave a great sigh of relief and prayed that she would never set eyes on His Grace of Stratford again.

CHAPTER 9

Diana's relief was short-lived. Not fifteen minutes after Stratford's departure, he was back again, his carrick and beaver hat white with snow.

"I fear, Miss Landane, that I must impose a little longer on your hospitality. One of my horses stumbled in a drift and has gone lame. Even without that mishap, however, I doubt that I would have been able to continue. The roads are already very nearly blocked by drifts. It may be some days before they are passable again.''

Diana suppressed a groan of dismay. She was so desperate to be rid of the duke, and now she was stuck with him, perhaps for days. How in the world was she to entertain him? The full burden would fall on her that day because her father, who was suffering from a monumental hangover, was unlikely to emerge from his bedchamber. Mrs. Cottam, too, was still abed with her nerves. Still, Diana's knowledge that she no longer had to fear that the duke might make her an offer calmed her own nervousness and brightened her spirits. ''I am sorry, Your Grace. I know you find the prospect of being snowbound here dreadful.''

''Dreadful? No,'' he said carelessly as Topham, the butler, helped him from his carrick. ''If one must be stranded in a country house during a storm, better it to be one as comfortably run as yours.''

She was certain he was being satirical. ''I am sorry that Greycote displeases Your Grace,'' she told him stiffly, wondering what hilarious tales he would tell of it when he returned to London.

The duke looked at her sharply. ''I was paying you a compliment—a sincere one.''

To cover her surprise, she said hastily, ''I fear father will not be down today. He is under the weather.''

The duke looked both relieved and alarmed. ''Nothing serious, I hope.''

''You need not fear it being contagious,'' she replied tartly. ''It is caught only from a bottle.''

Stratford chuckled. ''Yes, he did make very heavy indentures yesterday.''

Topham had disappeared with the duke's carrick and beaver hat, but His Grace and Diana were still standing in the entry hall. Recollecting her duties as hostess, she asked, "Would you like tea?"

"I'd like nothing better."

Diana ordered it and led the duke into the drawing room, where he warmed his hands at the fire.

In an impressively short time, Topham arrived with a heavy silver tray, bearing the tea service, bread and butter, scones and clotted cream, and a dish of blackberry jam.

The duke watched Diana as she poured tea into a cup for him. "You must get dreadfully bored here, Miss Landane."

She shook her head. She loved Greycote's peace and quiet after her unhappy memories of her London season. She appreciated, too, the time she had to devote to her painting and gardening. Although she missed Eliza and Mary Prentice, there was still George to accompany her on long rides and walks. "I much prefer life in the country to that of London."

"Why?"

She handed the duke his cup of tea and smiled. "If you have to ask the reason, you could never understand it."

The answer seemed to startle him. "Are you a recluse, never going to London?"

"Hardly a recluse, Your Grace, nor do I avoid London. Only London society. The city itself I visit two or three times a year to shop and see the latest plays. I am very fond of the theater."

He had lifted his cup to his lips and was studying her over its rim. "What have you against London society?"

"I find it most tiresome. All those bored gentlemen, like you, who cannot gamble away their fortunes fast enough."

He grinned. "But I am not given to gambling."

"So there is one vice you have not acquired."

The grin vanished. He lowered his cup and stared at her. "I beg your pardon," he said in that icy tone of his that never failed to reduce a hostess to a quivering apprehension.

But Diana was unaffected. In fact, she was quite enjoying giving him a dose of the blunt tongue that he was so good at inflicting upon others. "Your reputation as a rake, my lord duke, is quite notorious."

Stratford's arched right eyebrow shot up. "Is it? I fear I am ill informed on the subject."

"One's reputation is rarely discussed to one's face."

"I have not noticed many women frightened away by it," Alexander said dryly.

"No doubt some women find it more a challenge than a deterrent."

"But not you?" The duke's arched right eyebrow soared to a new height of skepticism. "I am surprised, Miss Landane. You seem like a woman who would enjoy a challenge."

"Only worthwhile challenges," she said sweetly, giving him a disarming smile, which, to her surprise, he returned.

"Now that you have demolished me and all the other men in London, what is your appraisal of the women?"

"Oh, I find them quite as tiresome as the men. Their only concern beyond their new gowns is their vouchers to Almack's. They curry the favor of that old dragon Lady Jersey." Diana screwed up her face, pretended to study Stratford through an imaginary quizzing glass, and said in a pinched voice that mimicked Lady Jersey's, "I believe Miss Landane wants conduct, and her gown is not at all the thing. We cannot permit her here again."

Stratford laughed in delight at this deadly accurate imitation of the old dragon of Almack's.

"I shall never understand why it is thought to be such a treat to be permitted in Almack's," Diana said. "It is always hot and crowded, the sandwiches are usually stale, and the lemonade is terrible."

The duke laughed again. "My own sentiments exactly. At least, Miss Landane, we agree on something."

"But on nothing else, I am sure," she retorted sharply.

He studied her thoughtfully, toying absently with the handle of his cup. "I believe that I recently met an admirer of yours, Gilfred Sillsby."

She could not repress a laugh. "He is no admirer of mine, I assure you."

"I apprehend that you do not like him."

"He is a fool."

The duke's haughty right eyebrow raised again in a question mark. "But I understand that he wished to marry you."

"I told you that he was a fool."

The duke look so startled that Diana could not repress a smile. "'Twas not me that he wished to marry but my fortune."

Stratford lifted his cup to his lips, again studying her over its rim. "Perhaps you underestimate your charms." He took a sip from his cup.

"I have none."

Alexander choked and hastily returned his cup to its saucer. "Rather hard on yourself, aren't you?"

She shrugged. "Merely honest."

"I have known many women, Miss Landane, who overestimated their attractions but never one who so underestimated them."

She glared at him. He was such a confirmed rake that he felt he had to charm every woman he met, even one like her who disgusted him. Irritation edged her voice as she said, "Now I see why you have enchanted so many women with your silver tongue, my lord duke. You need not waste it on me, however. I am immune."

Stratford stared at her, his silver tongue failing him for some moments.

Diana smiled at him sweetly.

Finally, he said, "Just as you were immune to Sillsby's lovemaking?"

"Lovemaking!" She burst out laughing at the memory.

The duke's eyebrow arched haughtily. "What is so amusing?"

Quite forgetting herself, Diana jumped up, pulled out the puffed sleeves of her gown, and sucked in her waist to emulate Sillsby's padded shoulders and laced-in waist. Then she mimicked his diffuclty with his viselike collar and corset as he tried to kiss her hand.

The duke dissolved in laughter. When he recovered, he said, "I suppose he plied you with compliments."

"With lies!" Diana corrected him. In a wicked imitation of Sillsby's effusive tones, she said, "My dear Miss Landane, what beautiful coloring you have. Quite out of the ordinary."

By now, the duke was regarding her with considerable interest. "But I understand that your father favored the match with Sillsby."

"Father would favor any match, but particularly one with a fortune hunter as desperate as Sillsby."

"Why? One would think that is precisely the sort of man your father would wish to protect you from."

"To the contrary. He offers Father the best hope of getting some of the fortune my grandfather left me. In exchange for his consent, Father undoubtedly extracted the promise of a sizable sum from Sillsby."

"I gather you are averse to marriage," the duke said quietly. "Why?"

Diana stared out the window. The snow was falling hard, and it was being whipped into a biting fury by the wind that nearly obliterated the world beyond the window. Diana could scarcely make out the vague outline of the great elm not twenty feet beyond the drawing-room window. "It should be quite obvious to so astute an observer as you, my lord duke, that the only possible interest a man could have in such a drab as me is my fortune."

His piercing gray eyes were studying her again. "Is it?" he asked, a sardonic smile playing on his lips.

Diana was beginning to find the conversation and his scrutiny uncomfortable. She wondered apprehensively what she was to do with him for the rest of the day. "Perhaps you would like to peruse Greycote's library," she said hopefully. "It is modest, but you may find a volume to your liking."

The duke's lips twitched. "I am afraid that you shall not be rid of me so easily, Miss Landane. I am not at all in the mood for reading. Perhaps you will indulge me in a game of ombre or piquet."

Diana was dismayed, but her sense of duty as a hostess outweighed her dread of Stratford, and she consented to ombre.

To her surprise, the day passed far more quickly than ever she could have imagined it would. Stratford, with his smooth skill of tongue, soon had Diana in a discussion of a particularly memorable performance, which both had seen, of Mrs. Siddons as Lady Macbeth.

The conversation drifted to mutual acquaintances. Alexander was soon laughing heartily at Diana's gift for mimicry, which was unerring in skewering affectations.

"Now I see why Alexander Pope is such a favorite of yours," the duke said after a remarkable imitation by Diana of Lord Twitham and the silly pronouncements he delivered in a portentous voice. "You are as clever a satirist as he is."

At dinner, Landane was still indisposed, although Mrs. Cottam made an appearance, torn between her nervous terror at the thought of actually eating with the duke of Stratford and her duty to Diana, who on no account should be permitted to dine alone with such a disreputable man.

This view much amused Diana, since she had just spent the day alone with that wicked man. His conduct had given her no cause for concern, but his charm had. It was clear to her now why so many women found him irresistible. She was not yet one of their number, but she had to admit that he made a most entertaining companion.

Although Mrs. Cottam made it to the table, she was so awed by Stratford that she could scarcely utter a word. Nevertheless, the meal went considerably better than the previous evening's disaster. A relaxed Diana, secure in the knowledge that nothing on earth would move Stratford to make an offer for her, engaged in lively discussions with him.

When the meal was concluded, Alexander took Mrs. Cottam's arm, a gesture that very nearly precipitated a relapse in the awed woman. As he led her into the drawing room, he asked, "Why does Miss Landane always wear such drab, unbecoming clothes?"

"But she doesn't. She—" Mrs. Cottam broke off in confusion.

"She what?" the duke prompted.

The old lady turned scarlet beneath her rouge. "She has some pretty gowns," she said lamely.

In the drawing room Diana said, "I am at a loss to know how to entertain you, Your Grace. Perhaps you would like to play more ombre."

Stratford nodded his head toward the harp in the corner. "You could favor me with another concert."

She saw the amusement flickering in the gray eyes. "You are laughing at me."

"Quite the contrary. I am quite intrigued to see if you can duplicate your singular performance of last night. If you can, I shall be able to laugh, too, now that I know the joke. You see, I am not quite as stupid as you think me."

"I do not think you at all stupid, Your Grace, only arrogant."

He smiled, unperturbed. "How complimentary you are. You are quite as blunt as my mother was."

Diana sat down at the harp and performed as beautifully as she had that morning. Sometime later she glanced at the duke and saw that his eyes were closed. Thinking him asleep, she stopped abruptly and rose from the instrument.

His gray eyes opened.

"I thought I had lulled you to sleep."

"Only to contentment," he said with a disconcertingly warm smile.

CHAPTER IO

By the next day the worst of the storm had passed. Although a light snow still fell, the wind had died away, leaving behind giant snowdrifts like great white sand dunes. Diana knew from their size that there was no hope the roads would be passable and the duke could leave.

Again, the burden of entertaining him would fall on her. She silently cursed her father. Although he had recovered from his overindulgence, he was now catching cold, no doubt from his foolishness in having ridden out to meet Stratford on such a bitterly cold day. For some reason Diana could not fathom, her father was decidedly fearful of suffering from a red, runny nose and racking cough during the Owsleys' visit. He had announced he would remain abed to try to stave off his incubating illness.

Diana was in her private retreat at the back of the house, seated at her writing table, revising menus for the duke's extended stay.

"I thought I might find you here."

The duke's voice startled Diana. She looked up from the menus spread before her. He was standing in the doorway, resplendent as always in a frock coat, its skirt pleated in back, of finest blue broadcloth. His waistcoat was of pale blue watered silk with an embroidered border of white flowers.

Annoyance flashed in her eyes that he would dare to invade her sanctum. Then she remembered her eyeglasses, which lay on the table, and hastily put them on.

"Why not leave those dreadful spectacles off?" the duke said.

"I have told you that I am blind without them."

"Are you now?" he asked blandly. "You seemed to be doing quite well without them just now. You do not look in the least happy to see me."

"I cannot say that I am."

"Why not?" he challenged, stepping uninvited into the room and looking about him. "What a delightful room!" he exclaimed.

His roving eye stopped abruptly when he saw her cherished bust of Hamlet, which depicted the Danish prince as he was frozen in indecision, tormented by his doubts. The duke started visibly and demanded roughly, "Where did you get that?"

Diana, nonplussed by the harshness of his voice, followed his gaze to the sculpture. "Isn't it magnificent?" she asked proudly. "It is my favorite piece and a Christmas gift."

"From an admirer?" Alexander demanded.

She laughed, her voice as limpid as her harp. "I have no admirers."

He spun around. "Most women would not admit that for the world."

"I am not most women."

The gray eyes glinted strangely. "Most decidedly you are not. You still have not told me who gave you the bust."

She rose from her desk and walked over to it. "I saw it when I was in London shopping before Christmas. I quite fell in love with it. The owner wanted a most shocking price, considering it is by an unknown sculptor, but I was wild to have it. My trustee, Mr. Pearce, knowing that, contrived to buy it for me as a Christmas present from my grandfather's estate. Under the will, Mr. Pearce cannot give me money until I marry, but he can buy me Christmas and birthday gifts." She touched the bust lovingly. "See how Hamlet's frustration and despair and indecision are so clear in the face. Isn't it a superb piece?"

"It is interesting," Alexander said noncommittally.

His tepid response to such a fine work angered her. "Interesting! It is quite as good as anything John Flaxman has ever done."

For some reason, the duke seemed uncomfortable. "What do you know of the sculptor?" he asked, still not committing himself to the worth of the piece.

"It's all very mysterious. He uses the name Lysipus, which, of course, must be a pseudonym derived from the Greek sculptor Lysippus."

The duke, who still appeared severely discomforted, said nothing.

"What is it you find fault with?" Diana burst out, hurt by what she took to be his silent criticism and ready to do battle on behalf of her prized acquisition. "You need not worry about wounding my feelings with your assessment, for I am certain that I can prove your complaints worthless."

"Is Hamlet your favorite character from Shakespeare?" the duke asked hastily, seeming eager to switch the subject from the work's merits.

A mischievous gleam that not even the thick glass of her

spectacles could hide sparkled in Diana's eyes. "No, Portia is my favorite."

The duke laughed. "I might have guessed." He walked over to a painting on the wall, a luminous landscape of a lake shimmering like silver as the sun faded behind the trees that lined the shore. In the lower right corner were the same intertwined initials that he had seen on several other paintings he had admired at Greycote. "Who is this painter whose works you favor? He did the landscape in my room, the one of the Bath crescent in the sitting room, and several others. Is he another one of your great discoveries?"

It was Diana's turn to be discomforted. Although she could detect no note of sarcasm in the question, she was certain it was intended. Her cheeks burned as she said in a small voice. "You do not like the paintings, either?"

"Don't be silly," he said brusquely. "The artist has enormous talent. Who is he?"

His unexpected praise only heightened her embarrassment. "I am sorry to disillusion you, Your Grace, but the paintings are mine."

"You did this?" He turned from the landscape, regarding her with new interest. "You handle light brilliantly."

"You are most kind, Your Grace," she replied stiffly. "You need not be."

"I am not being kind at all, you silly goose." His gray eyes examined Diana with such intensity that she was unnerved. Suddenly, he reached up and ran his finger lightly along her cheek.

She gasped and drew back, shocked at his effrontery. "How dare you?"

His eyes gleamed with amusement. "But my dear Miss Landane, you have already informed me what an utterly disreputable man I am. I should not have wanted to disappoint you." He pulled out a spotless white handkerchief and carefully wiped his finger on it, leaving a yellow stain on the fine linen.

Diana, unnerved by this turn of events, cried angrily, "You are outrageous. Go away and leave me alone."

"No," he said languidly. "I shall not."

"What? How rude you are!"

From his surprised look, Diana knew that no one had ever dared call the duke of Stratford rude to his face before.

"No, Miss Landane, it is you who are rude," he replied in that same languid voice that infuriated her. "I am your guest, and it is your duty to entertain me."

"You are not my guest, my lord duke," she said angrily. "You are my father's."

"But I am told he is still indisposed. And you would be a very poor hostess indeed if you did not step into the breach."

"You are insufferable," she snapped, unable to keep from her face her dismay at the thought of having to entertain him for the rest of the day.

Seeing her look, the duke said with amusement, "Oh, come, am I such a bore as all that?"

"Even as harsh a critic of Your Grace as I cannot accuse you of being a bore," Diana admitted.

"Then, since nature has conspired to trap us here together, let us contrive to have a mutually pleasurable time of it."

Again, Diana was astonished at how quickly that day and the next—for the snowdrifts still blocked the road—passed in Alexander's company. He displayed a lively interest, although she was certain it was feigned, in her life at Greycote and her opinions on a variety of subjects. This led to a discussion of art, about which—to Diana's great surprise—the duke was extremely knowledgeable.

From art they turned to furnishings, and he again complimented her on Greycote.

"I had the pleasure of visiting your grandfather's house in London once," Alexander said. "He and I shared a taste for fine French furniture. He had the most magnificent collection I had ever seen outside of Versailles before the Revolution."

"You saw Versailles back then?" she exclaimed. "How wonderful it must have been."

He nodded and began entertaining her with amusing anecdotes about his travels.

Once, when she stood up and went to the fireplace to stir up the embers, she caught him staring at her intently.

"Why are you watching me like that?" she asked bluntly. "One would think I am attractive, which I am not."

"But you have a lovely figure and the good sense not to ruin it with corsets and stays."

Although he spoke seriously enough, Diana was certain his words reflected mocking disapproval of her failure to properly corset herself.

"However," he continued, "I do wonder why you insist on wearing such drab clothes."

"I like them," she lied. In truth, she detested them. It was always such a great relief when her father left Greycote and she could go back to the stylish pastel gowns she favored.

"I don't believe you," the duke said flatly.

"Why not?"

"You like color too much in your paintings to espouse such drabness in your clothes."

She was dumbfounded. The duke was demonstrating disconcerting perceptiveness.

At breakfast the next morning, the duke announced that his groom had checked the roads and found them at last passable. He would be departing from Greycote shortly.

Landane, whose appearance at the breakfast table marked the first time that he had been seen since the night of Stratford's arrival, tried to persuade His Grace to stay. The duke was adamant. As he rose from the table, he requested a private audience with Landane.

Diana returned to her private preserve. She felt a pang of regret that Stratford was departing. He had been such good company the past three days that it would seem dull with him gone. "What a silly fool you are to let him charm you so easily," she told herself as she sat down at her writing desk to draft a reply to Antoine's letter. The words to Antoine, however, did not come easily. Fifteen minutes later, when Stratford suddenly appeared in the door, she had scarcely gotten beyond the first paragraph.

Diana supposed the duke had come to bid her farewell. She rose from her writing table, carefully slipping a blank sheet of paper over the one on which she had been writing to Antoine.

The duke seemed strangely agitated. His face looked uncertain, as though he were confronted by an unhappy and perplexing task. He studied her silently with a piercing, critical gaze as his fingers toyed with the silver buttons of the fine brown frock coat, perfectly tailored to his muscled body. He seemed to be searching for words he could not find. His strange demeanor baffled Diana.

Suddenly, without preamble, he told her in a strained voice, "I have decided to marry you."

The world whirled about her. She feared that for the first

time in her life she might faint. Recovering, she stared aghast at him. "You are joking!"

"Don't be a featherhead," he snapped. "I am not in the habit of joking about a subject as serious as that."

His handsome face was stern and unhappy. Even in her anger she could not deny that he cut a fine figure. He could have had his pick of London debutantes. This thought only reassured her that the sole possible attraction she could hold for him was her money, which he would lavish upon his mistresses. It occurred to her that he no more liked having to make his offer than she liked receiving it. He had to be even more desperate than she could have imagined.

Her own temper ignited, and her eyes flashed with fury. "Well, my lord duke, I have decided *not* to marry you."

From the look on his face, it was clear to Diana that he was even more thunderstruck by her rejection than she had been by his announcement.

Her anger mounted. It had never occurred to him that any woman would reject his suit, least of all a poor drab like her. He had not even made the feeblest attempt to woo her. Instead, he had addressed her, she thought, as he might have one of his chattels. It was monstrous. Undoubtedly, he had expected her to be both pathetically grateful and ecstatically happy at the prospect of becoming his wife and duchess— and of escaping spinsterhood in the bargain. Why should it matter to her that he cared not a whit about her, only about her fortune? She seethed with rage at his arrogance and conceit.

"Your father has given his consent," the duke told her.

"I am certain he has! He would give his consent to the first beggar that walked by."

His gray eyes grew dark and ominous as storm clouds. "I am hardly a beggar. Nor was I aware that an offer from me was so repulsive. I can name a long list of beauties who would be overjoyed."

"Then, my lord duke, I suggest that you ask one of *them* and spare me the great honor. And it is an enormous honor, isn't it, my lord duke, that someone of your great consequence should offer for such an antidote as me who has nothing at all to recommend her but a mere hundred thousand a year."

His gray eyes regarded her incredulously. "Are you accusing me of marrying you only for your money?"

"That is precisely what I am accusing you of, my lord duke. I am afraid, however, that you must have been sadly misinformed on its size. It is not nearly so large as the British treasury!"

The duke started. "So young Whorton did tell you what I said to your father."

"Yes. Now I imagine you are going to swear to me that you never gave the slightest thought to the size of my fortune when you set out for Greycote."

"I am not going to lie to you, Diana, but—"

"My name, my lord duke, is Miss Landane," she interrupted coldly, paraphrasing the remark he had made to her father upon his arrival.

"My apologies, Miss Landane. I thought such a liberty was permissible with one's betrothed."

"We are not betrothed," she ground out. "I will not marry you."

He was as angry now as she was, and their eyes clashed like dueling swords. "May I point out to you that you are hardly a loser in this transaction? You will become the duchess of Stratford, with all the honor attendant on that position, the mistress of a great estate at Mistelay, and a person in the first rank of society." His gray eyes swept her insultingly. "That is quite a coup for—" He broke off.

"For one who has so little to offer so grand a man as you?" she cried. "You, my lord duke, are no better than

Gilfred Sillsby or any of the other fortune hunters my father has brought here."

A dull red flush of anger spread over his handsome face. "I think, Miss Landane, you shall discover on our wedding night that I am a much better bargain than that posturing fop Sillsby."

His smug certainty that he would pleasure her stung her into replying, "You are repugnant to me."

Her words seemed to snap the last vestige of his control. He stepped toward her, and Diana thought for a second he might strike her. Through clenched teeth, he said, "I can promise you, Miss Landane, that you would be the first in a very long line of women ever to voice that particular complaint."

Suddenly, he pulled her into his arms and kissed her hard. He so surprised her that she was helpless in his arms. Then she began to feel like Sleeping Beauty, awakening from a lifelong sleep beneath the kiss of her prince. Utterly pleasurable sensations, never before felt by her, coursed through her, rendering her even more helpless. Not even when Antoine had kissed her had it been like this. She surrendered to Alexander's kiss, hating herself for her weakness. Feeling her response to him, his kiss grew deeper, more passionate, more devastating. When at last he let her go, she was so shaken that she could only stare at him with wide eyes.

His gray eyes gleamed with triumph, and he said with a husky laugh, "You see; you'll have no complaints."

Diana's face burned with humiliation at how easily he had triumphed over her.

She pulled away from him, her eyes filled with anger, and lashed out, hardly knowing what she was saying in her fury. "What irony, my lord duke. How galling it must be to you, having at last succeeded in squandering your fortune on your many lovely amourettes, that you are now forced to offer for such a rich drab as I. But of course, it will generate a new fortune to squander on them.''

Stratford's face was white with fury. A vein stood out on his left temple, pulsing with his anger. ''You insult us both grievously.'' He stalked to the window and for a long time stared out at the snow-blanketed garden until he regained his control. When he turned back to her, a strange, hard look glinted in his eyes, and his voice was as cold as ice.

''I think, Miss Landane, we shall deal very well together. I need your money, and you need a husband to remove you from here and obtain your grandfather's fortune. I will make few demands upon you as my wife.''

''Only upon my money.''

He clenched his jaw in fury, but when he spoke it was with frigid calm. ''Only upon your money. If you do not like London, you may remain at Mistelay and refurnish it to your taste. I ask only that you run the household there as efficiently as you run Greycote. I will, of course, require children.'' His voice dripped with sarcasm. ''But given your response to my kiss, I do not think you will find the begetting of them entirely unpleasant.''

Diana had never felt so humiliated in her entire life. ''Please,'' she whispered in a choked voice. ''Get out of here and leave me alone.''

He gave her a slight bow. ''Gladly, Miss Landane.'' He stalked to the door and stopped. ''It pains be to be so disobliging to you, but marry me you will!''

As his steps retreated down the hall, Diana burst into tears of mingled rage, fear, despair, and confusion. How unspeakable it would be to be married to a man whose only interest was her fortune and who held her in such utter contempt.

Somehow she would, she must, escape him.

CHAPTER 12

Diana was still sobbing when Mrs. Cottam found her twenty minutes later. Much alarmed, for she had never seen the usually cheerful Diana cry like this before, Mrs. Cottam tried, in her fluttering, ineffectual way, to comfort her. It was some moments, however, before Diana could manage even to sob out the reason for her misery.

When finally Mrs. Cottam understood its cause, she asked in astonishment, "Marry Stratford? But my dear, why are you crying? It is a brilliant match. Just think, you will be a duchess."

"What does that signify when it means I shall be married to that horrid, odious man?"

"The duke?" Mrs. Cottam was plainly astonished. "But he is not at all odious. I have found him charming and polite, and you cannot deny he is very handsome."

"He is an unprincipled rake," Diana said, sobbing.

Mrs. Cottam's handkerchief fluttered helplessly in her hands. "I cannot believe now that I have met him that he is as bad as his reputation makes him out to be."

"He is worse," Diana cried. "He is nothing but a fortune hunter."

"Surely he cannot be marrying you only for your money. He must have plenty of his own. And if that is his motive, Mr. Pearce will refuse him just as he has refused all the others.

Diana shook her head sorrowfully. "No, Mr. Pearce will never refuse his permission to the duke. It is exactly the marriage that Grandpapa would have given his fortune to arrange for me, and Mr. Pearce knows that as well as I do." Diana clasped the older woman's hand. "No, if I am to escape the duke, I must do so on my own."

"What do you mean, escape? I pray, Diana, you do not do anything foolish."

Diana forced a smile, as false as it was reassuring, to her lips. "What could I do?" She dared take no one, not Mrs. Cottam, not even George Whorton, into her confidence. Both would resist the scheme that was forming in her head. She thought of the letter that she had started writing to Antoine. Thank God she had not had a chance to finish and send it. Now she would write him a very different letter.

Diana did not delude herself that she still loved Antoine. But it would be far better to marry a man that she had once loved than an arrogant rake whom she hated. She knew now what she must do. She would pretend to go along reluctantly with the wedding plans, but the smug, haughty duke would never meet her at the altar.

After Mrs. Cottam left her, Diana went back to her writing table and tore up the letter she had started to Antoine. Taking a fresh sheet of paper, she stabbed her pen into the inkwell and began a letter to Mr. Pearce. It was an impassioned plea to him to deny his approval to Stratford's suit. To it she appended every argument against the duke that she could think of. Even though she was determined to argue her case, she was certain that her letter would have no effect on her trustee. After all, it was her grandfather's wishes that he was bound to carry out.

She expected greater success with her second letter—this one to Antoine. She was still writing it when the Owsleys' arrival was announced. Hastily, she hid the partially completed letter in the drawer beneath her account books and went to greet her new guests.

As she passed a mirror by the door, she saw that her eyes were still red and swollen—indeed, her entire face was puffy—from her storm of weeping.

In the hall, she nearly bumped into George Whorton in his redingote.

Her ravaged face alarmed him. "Diana, what the devil is it?"

"Stratford has offered for me."

George's jaw dropped. "You're hoaxing me. He said he wouldn't—"

"Obviously he is desperate," she replied bitterly. "But what are you doing here?"

"Your new guests stopped at Beaconstone, seeking directions. Since they are strangers to these parts, I thought I had better guide them here. The drifts are so deep that it's difficult to tell where the road is in some spots unless you know it."

In the entry hall, Landane was hovering solicitously over Isabel Owsley, a petite girl of pale coloring and hair that fell around her narrow face in tight ringlets. Her lips were drawn into a seemingly perpetual pout. Despite this, she was a pretty creature with large blue-green eyes, which were her best feature. She gazed up at Landane with the sly look of a small child seeking her own way from an indulgent parent. She was complaining to him of the terrible state of the roads that she and her parents had been forced to travel to reach Greycote, of the horrid storm they had been caught in, of the dreadful inn where they had had to take refuge from the storm for two odiously dull days, and of the wretched deficiencies of her abigail.

Her parents hovered in the background behind her. Owsley was gray and portly, while his wife was a thin stick of a woman with a face that had the sharp severity of a hag about it.

Diana ordered tea to warm her guests after their cold journey. As she led them toward the drawing room, the duke, in his white, many-caped carrick, came down the stairs, followed by his valet, carrying two portmanteaus. The duke's eyes locked with Diana's, and he glared at her.

But the awkwardness of the moment was papered over by

an exclamation of delight from Isabel, who broke off her complaints, freed herself from Landane's arm, and rushed forward like an impetuous child who has just sighted her favorite personage.

"Your Grace," she cried, "what a happy surprise to find you here."

It was clear to Diana from the glowing look that Isabel gave Stratford that she was infatuated with him. It was equally clear from his cold, curt response that her interest was not reciprocated in the slightest. But Isabel was not to be discouraged. She assured the duke in effusive terms what a pleasure it was to see him. She feared that at that time of year Greycote would be most boring. But of course with him there, it could never be boring.

No wonder, Diana thought as she watched Isabel simper over the duke, that he was so conceited when it came to women.

The duke regarded Isabel coolly. "I fear I must disappoint you. I am just departing."

Isabel's pout grew more pronounced. "But you cannot desert us. Why, it would be rude to leave just as we arrived."

"Then rude I must be," His Grace responded blandly.

Isabel turned to Landane, her voice rising to a whine. "Surely you can persuade the duke to stay another day. It should be so much more enjoyable for me."

Landane looked less than happy about the whole conversation. Nor did he look in the least as though he wished his future son-in-law to remain another instant.

Diana, all too mindful of the painful scene that had just occurred between her and the duke, was hesitant to intervene, but finally she said timidly, "Perhaps Your Grace could be persuaded to take a cup of tea with us before you depart."

He looked at her sharply, his gaze taking in her swollen

face and eyes, then said with a dazzling smile that only Diana knew was false, "But of course *you*, my dear Miss Landane, could persuade me."

Isabel glared balefully at Diana.

In the drawing room, Isabel attempted to sit beside the duke, but he managed somehow to maneuver so that he was seated beside Diana, to the latter's enormous discomfort.

Both Isabel and her mother studied the room so critically that Diana was astonished. Nor did they appear pleased with what they saw. Diana was not surprised at such a reaction, for she knew Lady Owsley was one of those women totally devoid of taste and flair who thought only in the most rigid clichés.

Landane, too, had been watching Isabel's scrutiny. "What do you think of it?"

Her pouting gaze swept the room. "I shall replace the wallpaper and the furniture as soon as we are married. It is far too insubstantial. I prefer Kent."

The empty cup that Diana had just picked up from the tray fell from her hand into her lap. "Married?" she asked in bewilderment, her hand groping for the fallen cup.

Her father shifted uncomfortably in his chair. "I fear I neglected to tell you my happy news, Diana. Miss Isabel and I are to be married."

Diana, her cheeks stained red with embarrassment, could say nothing. Her realization that Stratford was intently watching her face increased her humiliation. For some reason, he looked furious. As the tense silence lengthened, she swallowed hard and said, "I wish you both happy."

Isabel did not even acknowledge the felicitation but plunged on about her plans to redecorate Greycote. "And, of course, these paintings—I detest landscapes—must go. Don't you agree, Your Grace?" She gave the duke her most coquettish smile."

"No," he snapped. His eyes glittered dangerously.

"Quite frankly, I would hate to see this room after you have destroyed it."

Isabel's pouting little mouth dropped open in amazement.

Diana said in a small, stricken voice, "I think it rather nice the way it is."

"But of course it won't be your home any longer." Isabel's voice was determined. "I know you will prefer to set up your own household elsewhere." Her tone rose to a shrill whine. "I think it is too, too unfortunate when spinsters insist upon imposing themselves upon their poor fathers simply because they are such frights they cannot possibly attract a husband."

Shocked silence reigned in the room. Diana struggled to hold back her tears.

"But of course she won't be living here," the duke said sharply. "I am afraid, Miss Isabel, you have not heard my own good news. Miss Landane is doing me the honor of becoming my wife."

Diana felt a flash of gratitude to Stratford.

Isabel examined Diana in disbelief, then burst out in a contemptuous laugh. "Her?" she said to the duke. "You are joking."

Isabel's voice was so scornful that Diana was embarrassed now for Stratford. How humiliating for anyone of his consequence to have his choice of bride so ridiculed.

"I have never been more serious in my life," the duke said firmly.

A note of derision sounded in Isabel's whine. "What on earth could you see in her?"

"Infinitely more than I can see in you," Stratford snapped.

Isabel gaped at him, then began to cry.

Landane finally stirred himself. "You Grace, I cannot permit you to insult—"

Stratford whirled on him. "You besotted fool. You have

only yourself to blame for this unpleasantness. Why didn't you have the decency to tell your daughter about your forth-coming marriage before you brought this rude little shrew into the house?''

Diana could stand it no longer. She rose, her face as white as chalk, and fled from the room. George jumped up and went after her. The duke gave a final withering glance at Landane, got up, and stalked into the hall, where he found George looking about helplessly, uncertain of where Diana had gone.

George regarded the duke with deep suspicion. ''Surely you are joking about marrying Diana.''

''As I told that ill-mannered little chit in there, I have never been more serious in my life.''

''No wonder Diana has been crying her eyes out.''

The duke's haughty right eyebrow shot up. ''I had not un-til today thought myself so repulsive a prospect as a hus-band.''

''But you are to Diana,'' George blurted out. ''She cares not a whit for titles and social position. She has always lived in terror that she would be forced to marry a man who wanted only her money and that he would make her life as miserable as her father made her mother's.''

''Her life will be considerably less miserable with me than it would be here with Isabel as mistress,'' Alexander said. He shook his head in disgust. ''If Landane thinks he has financial difficulties now, he will be truly confounded after Isabel's extravagances are substituted for his daugh-ter's careful management.''

''That may be true, Your Grace, but Diana knows that there can be no reason on earth why you would marry her except her money.''

''No reason on earth, George?'' Alexander said quietly. ''But it was you who told me that Diana was the only leg shackle you yourself could imagine taking.''

George blushed. "But I know her."

"Yes, and I have come to appreciate that indeed there is both less and more to her than meets the eye."

The duke turned on his heel and strode toward the door. George watched him go, a thoughtful look in his eye.

CHAPTER 13

After returning to London, the duke of Stratford's pride, still wounded by Miss Landane's distaste for him, was dealt another blow when he called upon Mr. Stanley Pearce in his office in Fleet Street. Pearce's dingy suite, which hardly reflected his fame as a brilliant barrister, consisted of three rooms, if the anteroom, no bigger than a closet, could be called a room. Stratford was not kept waiting there but was hurried through a second room in which were crowded clerks, files, and legal documents in haphazard confusion into a third, which was Pearce's private sanctum.

That Stratford was spared the anteroom wait that would have been the lot of any other caller did nothing to soothe his irritation that he had been required to go there instead of having Pearce attend him at Stratford House in St. James. The duke was used to the world coming to him at his convenience, not the other way around.

Pearce sat behind a massive, much-battered oak desk, its top strewn with papers in a most disorderly fashion. He was a thin, elderly man with a large head much out of proportion to his small body. This discrepancy was further emphasized by a great gray beard as bushy as his thick eyebrows over great burning black eyes that seemed to bore into one's very soul. How apt his surname was, Stratford thought as he settled himself in an uncomfortable wooden armchair across the desk from the old man.

Pearce had a reputation for being a no-nonsense barrister who went straight to the point, and he did so now in a voice raspy with age. "Your Grace is here to seek my approval of your marrying Miss Landane."

The duke, somewhat taken aback by this abruptness, nodded.

"What are your motives in wishing to marry her?"

Alexander stiffened but replied smoothly, "It is time, indeed past time, that I took a wife and produced an heir."

Pearce's thin fingers drummed impatiently on the battered desk top. "I did not ask you why you were marrying, but why you chose Diana."

"She suits me," the duke said languidly.

"I cannot see how. Besides, she most particularly dislikes you."

Alexander stared coolly at his interrogator. "I presume she has told you why."

"Yes, she has written me at great length, listing numerous reasons why you would make her a wretched husband. Among other things, she finds you arrogant and contemptuous, particularly in your treatment of women."

"No woman of my close acquaintance has ever complained of my treatment of her."

"And if you are even half what your reputation makes you to be, you have been closely acquainted with a considerable number."

"I am not here to discuss my morals," Alexander said icily.

"But I am." Pearce leaned back in his chair and examined Alexander keenly from beneath those bushy gray brows. "Not only am I Diana's trustee, but I am exceedingly fond of her. I shall not permit her to fall prey to a fortune-hunting rake, which is what she says you are."

The duke seemed bored by the discussion. "Her mother apparently convinced her that any man who would make her an offer must be only after her fortune. She did her daughter a disservice."

The old man locked his thin fingers together and said slowly, "Her mother's motives were good. They lived for a time in Switzerland with a childhood friend of Lady Landane's. There Diana met a young French émigré, the son of the comte de Couday. The comte had lost both his head and the family fortune in the Revolution. The son was a penniless, opportunistic young charmer. Diana, who had just turned sixteen, fell wildly in love with him, and he convinced her to elope with him." Pearce raised his thin hand to his mouth and gave a short hacking cough.

From outside could be heard the voice of a street vendor hawking his wares.

"Fortunately, Lady Landane learned of the plan and whisked Diana back to England," Pearce said. "Lady Landane was wise enough to know that Diana was too much in love with Antoine to ever fully believe the truth about him, so she never attacked him directly. Instead, Lady Landane tried to impress upon Diana the dreadful fate that awaited her if she married such a man." Pearce gave another hacking cough and fell silent.

"What happened to Antoine?" Alexander asked.

Pearce shrugged. "To my knowledge, Diana never heard from him again. Once she and her mama came back to England, he wasted no time marrying another heiress, a very rich one, but not rich enough for his extravagances. He deserted her when he had run through her money. She was carrying his child at the time and died two months later in childbirth."

"Does Diana know Antoine's story?" Alexander asked.

The old man shook his head. "No, I have never told her. She is so set against marriage that I thought it would only make her more so to find that the one man she had loved was exactly what she most fears in men." The old eyes narrowed. "I find it most extraordinary, Your Grace, that you wish to marry a woman whose major attribute is her fortune."

"For one who says he is fond of Diana, you don't seem to hold a very high opinion of her." The duke crossed his leg casually. "To say her only attribute is her fortune does her an injustice."

"Her, yes. You, no. I have made preliminary inquiries about you. You are drowning in debt, although I have not yet learned the reasons."

The duke's indifference gave way to anger. "You may stop prying. Neither my grandfather nor my father was the wisest financial guardian. The family fortune was severely reduced when I inherited it. Both my brother and I have wasted huge sums, he at the gaming tables and I in the boudoir."

"Under those circumstances, you surely do not expect me to believe that you suddenly offered for Diana, whom you did not even remember meeting, for any reason other than her money."

Stratford uncrossed his leg and set his foot down rather sharply on the bare wooden floor. But when he spoke, it was in a careless tone. "Mr. Pearce, I do not care what you think my motives are. Let me remind you that it will be a marriage of mutual benefit. She stands to gain considerably by our marriage, as well, including an honored title and access to her fortune. I am persuaded it is exactly the marriage her grandfather would have wanted her to make."

"Diana's letter begs me to save her and her fortune from

you. I fear, given your reputation, she has reason for concern."

The duke's gray eyes glittered angrily. "In that case, retain control of her capital and turn over only the income to me each year."

"Only the income?" The black eyes beneath the thick gray brows flashed. "That alone is larger than many fortunes."

"Then," the duke said coldly, "it may even be sufficient to maintain me in the style to which I am accustomed."

Pearce's face was stony with disapproval. "That hardly sounds like a bargain for Diana."

"She will be far better off with me, whatever my motives are," Alexander said. "Even she will soon realize that her position will be impossible after Landane marries mean little Isabel Owsley, who will delight in making Diana's life miserable."

Pearce threaded his fingers together. "We have not discussed the marriage settlement."

Alexander's right eyebrow arched skeptically. "I would not think that necessary, particularly if you are retaining control of her capital."

"I am an old man, and I want to make certain that Diana is protected for life. I insist upon a settlement."

"How much?"

Pearce, anticipating hard bargaining, threw out an extravagant demand for starters.

Alexander shrugged. "Very well. Draw up the papers and I shall sign them."

Seeing Pearce's astonishment, Alexander said, "Did it not occur to you, sir, that I might want to see my wife protected, too?" He rose from his chair. "It appears that I have your approval to marry Diana."

"Yes."

The duke's handsome face was expressionless. "Good. I

know there is also a substantial dowry. Since I am presently quite short of ready cash, I shall need most of it very quickly to take care of some pressing obligations.''

Pearce flushed angrily. ''You are an arrogant bastard, Your Grace.''

The duke grinned. ''Arrogant, I grant you, but definitely not a bastard.''

CHAPTER 14

By the time the Owsleys departed from Greycote, Diana would have been the first to agree with Stratford that it would be impossible for her to remain there with Isabel as its mistress. In fact, that young lady had conducted herself during her stay as if she already were its mistress, giving imperious and unreasonable orders to the servants, planning in detail her tasteless redecoration schemes, and treating Diana as if she were a servant there only to do Isabel's petulant bidding. If Diana was slow to comply, her father was quick to chastise her rather than to defend her from his future wife's egregious demands.

Even then, Diana's situation would have been much worse had it not been for her betrothal to the duke and the restraining presence of Lady Owsley, who was both more ambitious and more astute than her spoiled daughter. Diana's formidable betrothed had already demonstrated he could be savage in his defense of his future wife, and Lady

Owsley recognized that to anger the duke could mean social suicide for her daughter.

The day after the Owsleys, accompanied by Lord Landane, had departed, Diana was in her little retreat at the back of the house. Sitting by the window, she was working on a landscape as cheerless as the frozen world outside when Mrs. Cottam came in, all aflutter with the news that a messenger from Stratford had arrived with two letters.

Handing them to Diana, Mrs. Cottam told her, "The messenger—he's in the duke's own livery of green and gold—says he is on no account to leave until he has your answer to the duke's letter."

The first of the two letters was from Mr. Pearce, informing Diana that he had given his consent to her marriage to Stratford.

"I need not tell you," Mr. Pearce wrote, "that this match would have pleased your grandfather enormously. Although I know it does not please you at the moment, I think the duke will prove to be an excellent mate for you."

Until that moment Diana had always thought old Mr. Pearce one of the shrewdest and wisest of men, but now she wondered bitterly if he had become senile. "An excellent mate!" she exclaimed in disbelief to Mrs. Cottam.

As if anticipating her protest, his next paragraph read: "In view of your concern about your fortune, you will be relieved to learn that His Grace has agreed that I should retain control of your capital unless you wish to stipulate otherwise. He has also agreed to a most generous marriage settlement."

"A marriage settlement." Diana looked up from the letter. "So that is how he fooled Mr. Pearce. I am amazed, however, that Stratford agreed to either stipulation. He is even more desperate than I thought."

Mrs. Cottam kneaded her hands nervously. "What will you do now? Mr. Pearce was your last hope."

"What can I do?" Diana asked with a meekness that would have worried Mrs. Cottam had she been a more intelligent and perceptive woman. Diana folded Mr. Pearce's letter slowly. "I cannot stay here after Father marries Isabel, and I have no money to set up a household of my own until I marry. Nor can I fight Father, Mr. Pearce, and the duke—all three of them. I have no choice but to marry Stratford."

Diana hoped that she sounded suitably resigned to the marriage, for she was, in fact, far from it. She had already written Antoine that she would meet him at the Red Fox Inn on February fifteenth and that they must flee the country together immediately, preferably on the same vessel that would bring him to England, if it could be arranged. If they did not escape abroad immediately, she would be torn from him as her mother had been torn from her lover, and she would be forced to marry Stratford.

Diana knew that when she married Antoine she would be forever relinquishing her grandfather's enormous fortune. Mr. Pearce would never give his consent to Antoine, particularly not after the duke's offer.

She had written Antoine frankly of the terms of her grandfather's will, which would leave her penniless when she eloped with him, but she had assured him that she did not care in the slightest about losing the money.

She would, she thought now as she opened the second letter that the duke's messenger had brought, do anything to escape Stratford. She still burned with shame at the insulting marriage of convenience he proposed and at his contempt for her. She could not suppress a little gleam of satisfaction at the thought of how humiliated he would be when the world learned he had been jilted by his dowd of a betrothed. All she had to do was find a way to get to the coast on February fifteenth.

The second letter was written on expensive stationery,

and the duke's crest was embossed at the top. It was a terse note, in Stratford's own hand, informing Diana that the notice of their betrothal had been published that morning in the *Gazette* and that they would be wed at Greycote on a date six weeks hence.

"So soon?" Mrs. Cottam exclaimed.

"Obviously he is in urgent need of my money," Diana said, fingering the heavy paper thoughtfully.

"But why are you to be married here instead of London?" Mrs. Cottam was enormously disappointed, her face looking like that of a child who had just been denied a favored toy. "I had so hoped that you would be married in London with all the great swells attending."

Diana could scarcely repress a shudder at the thought of such a dreadful charade played out for a skeptical and amused audience.

"My sister would have been so impressed," Mrs. Cottam wailed.

"The fastidious duke of Stratford would not like above half to display to the world a bride as unattractive as I." Diana could not keep the sarcasm from her voice. "He prefers to marry me quietly here, beyond the eyes of his critical peers."

Mrs. Cottam, unnerved by Diana's bitterness, hastily changed the subject. "What else does the duke say?"

Diana looked down at his dramatic black scrawl and read, "I have already ordered your wedding gown and trousseau, because my taste in such matters may be better than yours."

She looked up in anger. "His arrogant high-handedness is beyond belief. Not only am I to have no say in when or where I am to be married, but I am not even permitted to choose my gown or my trousseau. The conceited, insufferable . . ." She could find no noun strong enough to describe the duke and was reduced to sputtering in rage. It was some minutes before she was sufficiently calm to read the rest of the short note:

" 'Your presence will be required in London within the next month for fittings. Please notify my messenger of the day that you will arrive in London so that I may make the appointments.' "

A sudden smile sprang to her lips, and she hurried into the hall to tell the young messenger, quite splendid in his green-and-gold livery, "Inform the duke that I shall arive in London on the night of February fourteenth for fittings on the morning of the fifteenth."

She turned away, her mind still plotting furiously. London would put her that much closer to the coast. She would have no trouble reaching it by nightfall if she set out when she pretended to go to her fittings. It would be hours before she was missed, and even then no one would have the slightest idea of where to begin searching for her.

As she rejoined Mrs. Cottam, the older woman said, "The servants are in such a state. They all say they will give notice the moment that dreadful Isabel becomes mistress here."

"Yes, I know." Diana sat down before the bleak landscape on which she was working. "They all have come to me privately to ask if I could take them on at Mistelay."

"Could you?"

Diana studied her canvas with seeming intensity. Only she knew that she would never be mistress of Mistelay, and she did not want to raise false hopes in her servants only to have them bitterly disappointed. "I don't know," she finally said lamely.

"Will you ask the duke?"

"We'll see."

Two weeks later George Whorton stopped at Greycote on his way home from the village, bearing a fat letter for Mrs.

Cottam, whom he found in a state of acute nervousness over the prospect of accompanying Diana to London for her fittings.

"I shall have to go with her to London, of course," she complained, twisting her white linen handkerchief in her hands. "But you know how particularly I detest traveling. I am quite certain that I shall be prostrated in my bed for at least two days after my arrival, if we reach London alive."

George, who knew Mrs. Cottam's fear of traveling was as great as it was irrational, said lightly, "I assure you the roads these days are quite safe and very passable."

"Safe, perhaps, for a strong young man like you, but it is quite a different story for two defenseless women like Diana and me."

"Would you like me to accompany you?"

Mrs. Cottam looked as though George had just rescued her from a band of highwaymen. "I cannot tell you how grateful I should be if you would."

George smiled. "My pleasure. I've been looking for an excuse to go to London." He pulled a letter from inside his coat. "By the way, the post brought you a letter."

Mrs. Cottam seized it and gave a cry of delight. "It is from my sister, Mrs. Wise." Quickly, Mrs. Cottam broke the seal and scanned the letter.

"Oh, listen," she cried to George in a voice brimming with excitement. "My sister writes that Diana's betrothal to Stratford is the talk of London." Diana slipped unnoticed into the room as Mrs. Cottam began to read aloud the contents to George:

"'Everyone is astonished by the news, for it was thought the duke was beyond the age where he would take a wife—and then to have him ignore all the London beauties for a woman who resides in the country. The ton can talk of nothing else. You must write me, dear sister, and tell me more about Miss Landane, for she is the subject of intense curiosity. She is remembered as a plain, fat creature, and not at all the sort the duke would look at twice.

" 'It's said the person most shocked by the betrothed is Lady Bradwell, the duke's current convenient and a remarkable beauty. It's said she fainted upon hearing of it. But apparently she and the duke are reconciled, for she was seen at the theater two nights ago wearing a new emerald necklace that puts the crown jewels to shame. Lady Bradwell announced the necklace had been a present that very day from the duke.' "

A sob escaped from Diana. Both George and Mrs. Cottam whirled around at the sound.

"Oh, my dear Diana," the woman exclaimed as she saw Diana's ashen face. "I had no idea you were here."

George broke in, his voice like iron. "Mrs. Cottam, please go and leave me alone with Diana."

The woman scurried away.

Diana turned bitter eyes to George. "You see, Stratford plans to continue with that woman after we are married. She shall reap more benefit from my fortune than I ever shall. My money no doubt paid for her necklace."

George's square, honest face was troubled. "I think you do the duke an injustice, Diana."

Her face flushed with indignation. "He has just given his mistress an emerald necklace fit for a queen, but he has not given me even so much as the slightest paste token to mark our betrothal."

"I did not think you cared a fig about jewels."

"I don't. I would rather have my bust of Hamlet, but that is not the point. The duke cares nothing about me."

"I do not think he is as uncaring toward you as you insist," George retorted, meeting her angry gaze with thoughtful eyes. "Remember the trimming he gave Isabel Owsley for her conduct toward you."

"Yes." Diana's brows knitted in puzzlement. She had

been astonished that the duke had come so vigorously to her defense. It had been the first time during his stay at Greycote that he had unleashed the cruel tongue for which he was feared. The only conclusion she had been able to draw was that his arrogance would not permit him to let another insult his future duchess. However little he might think of her privately, he would allow no one to belittle her publicly.

"I think the duke is far more perceptive about you than you realize," George said.

Diana felt the pressure of his hand on her arm. Looking up, she saw he was studying her with worried eyes. "You have hatched some scheme, Diana. I know you have."

"Silly!" But even she knew her tone was unconvincing.

"I warn you, Diana. Don't do anything that you will regret the rest of your life. The duke is a determined man, and he means to marry you. You are a fool if you think that you can escape him, and you would be most unwise to try. Better that you try to fix his interest. I think you might even achieve a tolerably happy marriage."

"You call being neglected and ignored tolerably happy?" Diana cried.

"If you would but try, you might be agreeably surprised. But I know that if you fight him, you will find yourself in an even unhappier situation than your mother did. The duke is a far cry from the featherhead your father is."

Diana pulled away from George's grasp and turned her back on him.

"Take care, Diana, that you do not alienate Alexander forever with some foolish, doomed scheme."

CHAPTER 15

On the day of her departure for London, Diana picked for her journey the same ugly gray dress that she had worn to greet Stratford that day he had arrived at Greycote. Although she did not expect the duke to call upon her that night when she arrived in London, she took the precaution to make her complexion as sallow as she could manage from the clutter of jars on her dressing table. All in all, she thought with satisfaction as she regarded herself in the mirror, she looked particularly sickly and unattractive. The fastidious duke might well breathe a sigh of relief when he discovered she had fled him.

After George Whorton helped Diana and Mrs. Cottam into the coach and settled himself on the seat across from them, he studied Diana critically. "I am certain you meant to make yourself look uglier than you ever have before, Diana. May I congratulate you on succeeding so well."

"Thank you, George," Diana responded coolly.

"Diana, stop being such a ninnyhammer. Stop trying to do your best to repel the duke when you ought to be trying to make your peace with him."

Diana turned her head to the window, her lips compressed in a tight line, and said nothing.

A tense silence enveloped the coach. On the seat beside Diana, Mrs. Cottam, who considered the prospect of a ride to the next village a long and harrowing journey, was in a state of terror over the perils of the trip. Her overwrought nerves were further strained by an unexpected storm that struck shortly after the coach left Greycote. Her normal loquaciousness subdued by terror, she huddled in the corner of the coach, clutching at the strap as the coach slid about on the icy road.

Diana, too, was quiet, both because she was angry at George and because her mind was in turmoil. What if Antoine had not received her letter and was not at the Red Fox Inn? What if her escape plot went awry? She could not even bring herself to think what the consequences of that might be.

She was exceedingly nervous, too, about the prospect of seeing Stratford again. Whenever she thought of the last time that they had been alone together, her cheeks stained red. His searing kiss had proved to them both that she was far from immune to his attraction. Then there had been his rage. She understood enough of his pride and character to know that she had dealt him an unforgivable insult by trying to reject his suit. Since he had left Greycote, she had heard nothing from him save that one terse note. The silence did not bode well for their next meeting, which she fervently hoped would never come to pass. Unless he came to call that night, it would not, for on the morrow she would flee London and him.

The weather cleared for the final leg of their journey. Nevertheless, by the time the coach reached London, Mrs. Cottam was in such a state of nervous distress that she was certain to be abed not only the next day but the day after, as well. Although Diana did not wish Mrs. Cottam any discomfort, she had counted on the effects of the journey on the woman to aid in Diana's escape.

To Diana's dismay, Stratford was awaiting them when they arrived at Landane's house in Chesterfield Street. The duke had other engagements later in the evening. He was resplendent in black silk breeches with gilt buckles at the knees, a white satin waistcoat with sprigs and flowers embroidered on its edges and pocket flaps, and a coat of royal blue velvet. A single sapphire pin glittered in the folds of his elaborately arranged cravat. Once again, Diana was struck by how handsome he was.

Seeing his elegant attire, Diana regretted for an instant her own extreme dowdiness. Try as she might, she could not quite drive from her mind the unsettling memory of what it had been like to be held in those arms and kissed by those lips.

Equally unsettling to her was his affable greeting, accompanied by that famous smile of his and such solicitous concern for the difficulties of her journey that she found herself again weakening to his charm. There was not the slightest indication in his smooth friendliness that he remembered the rancor of their last scene alone at Greycote.

Having welcomed his betrothed, he turned to Mrs. Cottam, exclaiming, "You look as though you have had a dreadful trip."

His sympathy immediately won Mrs. Cottam, who loved nothing so much as commiseration. "I fear I shall be quite unable to leave my bed tomorrow to accompany Diana to her fittings. I suppose she will be safe with Tebbets." Her tone indicated that she was not at all sure of the coachman even though he had just managed to transport them safely to London.

"I shall be in the care of James, Father's London coachman," Diana said casually. "I gave Tebbets the morrow off. His sister here in London is very ill, and I told him he might visit her."

The duke turned to Diana. "I have selected a great many things for you."

Diana's temper flared. "I prefer to choose my own clothes."

Stratford was unperturbed. "Miss Landane, you are determined to provoke me. I am determined you shall not, and I am a most obstinate man."

"So I am learning. However, I shall dress as I please."

"No," the duke said quietly. "As my wife, you will dress to please me."

"You might have at least allowed me to choose my own wedding dress."

"Why?" he asked with a grin. "I have no desire to see my bride come to the altar in a black tent or some other equally original and fascinating creation."

Diana could not suppress a giggle. The duke took her arm gently, his touch producing a very pleasant but utterly disconcerting response in her. He guided her into a small sitting room where a huge box was resting on a table. Gesturing at the box, he said, "It is my betrothal present to you."

She opened the box, not knowing what to expect. To her astonishment, it yielded up a marble bust of Portia. She knew immediately that it had been done by the mysterious Lysipus. She gave a cry of delight, and her eyes sparkled with excitement behind the thick, wire-rimmed spectacles. It was a perfect companion piece to her cherished bust of Hamlet. Turning to the duke, she saw that he was watching her anxiously. "Wherever did you get it?" she asked.

"Do you like it?" Concern edged his voice.

"I love it."

Still, he seemed unconvinced. "I will buy you jewels if you wish, but I was persuaded that you might like this more."

She was both astounded and deeply touched by his perceptive reading of her. "You could not have given me anything that would have pleased me more." She smiled. "Truly, you could not have."

He smiled back and took her hands in his. "May I be permitted to call you Diana?"

She nodded, unable to find her voice as she looked up into his deep gray eyes, now as soft as velvet. His hands grasped her hands more firmly. "I swear to you, Diana, that you will never regret marrying me."

She could only stare at him. Her heart was beating so

quickly and loudly that she was certain he must hear it. She was slipping helplessly beneath the waves of his charm.

"Now I have a request of you, Diana," he said softly. "Will you grant it?"

Diana, who felt herself mesmerized by those gray eyes, was immediately back on her guard. No doubt he needed money. "What is it?"

He smiled down at her; it was a gentle, patient smile quite out of character with his usual demeanor of cool disdain. "I have never yet seen what my bride looks like." He reached up with his finger and rubbed at the yellow makeup on her cheek. "On the morrow I should like to see the real Diana Landane, who hides behind eyeglasses she does not need, sallow makeup, and hair powdered and worn like a grandmother's."

She stared at him, her eyes wide with astonishment. "I don't know what you mean," she said falteringly.

"You, my dear Diana, are a wretched liar. And I am a very impatient man." There was a determined gleam in his eyes. "If, upon my arrival here tomorrow night, I find you still concealing yourself, I shall personally scrub you clean of this fraud." He held up his fingers, stained yellow by her makeup. "I trust we understand each other."

Bereft of speech, she could only nod.

"Good." He smiled, gave her hand a small squeeze, and took his leave, saying, "I know you have had an exhausting trip and must be up early tomorrow for your fittings."

After his departure, she climbed the steps to her room in great confusion, which increased when she found in her bedchamber two large vases of yellow hothouse roses with a card from the duke that read simply, "Because you like them."

She sank down upon her bed, her mind whirling.

CHAPTER 16

Diana set out the next morning, ostensibly for her fittings, with James in the coach box. He was a dull-witted fellow with a gap-toothed grin who, she was certain, was too stupid to ever suspect what was afoot. When he stopped in front of the couturier's establishment in Bond Street and helped Diana down, she told him, "I shall be several hours, James. You might as well have yourself a pint while you are waiting. If you are back here by four, it should be soon enough."

He grinned, delighted at his dismissal, and urged the horses forward as Diana walked slowly toward the door of the shop. Once the coach rounded the corner, she stopped and turned back toward the street. She was wearing a black cloak and a huge unfashionable hat that covered all of her hair and hid her face with so many layers of net that even her father would not have recognized her.

A carriage, leather curtains drawn tightly across its windows to conceal its interior, drew up in front of her. Tebbets jumped down and handed her quickly into the vehicle, and they were on their way out of London.

It was not until they had left the city well behind that Diana unwrapped the yards of veiling that concealed her face, scrubbed clean of its yellow mask, and removed the huge hat. She had washed out the dulling rinse that she used on her hair, so that even in the deep gloom of the curtained coach its golden strands shone. She had left her steel-rimmed eyeglasses behind, too, on her dressing table with the pots of makeup. She would need them no more.

No one seeing her now would have recognized the lovely young woman as the same one who had arrived in Chesterfield Street the night before.

Less pretty, however, were her thoughts as the coach rushed across the English countryside, which had the brown tint of winter still upon it. Patches of grimy snow lay here and there. Instead of the exhilaration that Diana had felt at Greycote when she had contemplated her escape from Stratford, she now was only frightened and confused, her courage and her resolve shrinking like those patches of snow on the ground.

Her feelings for the duke had undergone a considerable change since her arrival in London the day before. She could find nothing at all in his conduct toward her the previous night to fault. He had been amiable, attentive, considerate, even tender. She remembered, too, what fun she had had with him during his brief stay at Greycote before his decision to marry her. She tried to tell herself that she was being a fool, that he had simply been charming her as he charmed every female he set his mind to. He was, she thought with bitterness at her own weakness, irresistible, for she had to admit to herself that she had come to care for him. How easily he had added her to his long list of conquests.

Yet she could not shake from her mind his anxious face as she had opened his gift to her. A large lump rose in her throat as she thought of his present. It had meant far more to her than emeralds, even diamonds, ever would have. Then there had been the roses. She was both pleased and a little frightened at how acutely perceptive of her he was. He had even seen through her disguise, something her own father had never tumbled to. George was right. Stratford was far from a fool.

She remembered his promise to her that she would not regret marrying him. She was stung by a pang of conscience. Now she was paying him back with treachery.

The coach passed a hedgerow of goat willows and spindle trees. Below them the white flowers of barren strawberry hung their heads.

And what of Antoine? As the coach drew Diana nearer to him, she grew more fainthearted. After all, she had not seen him for years. He was thirty now. How much had the years changed the young man she remembered? And what of his marriage? Diana had been eager to believe that her mother had written him of her nonexistent betrothal and that his heartbreak had precipitated his wedding. But was Antoine worthy of her trust?

Panic engulfed her. She could not go through with this mad scheme of hers. She would order Tebbets to turn the coach around and head back to London.

But then she remembered all that Antoine had risked to come to her side. She dared not fail him now when he had gambled even his life to see her. She was not so low a creature that she could abandon him under such circumstances. Much as she dreaded going through with their rendezvous, much as she longed to return to London, she must continue on.

She stared out the coach window at two dabchicks, still in their gray winter plumage, diving for fish on a small lake. She had a duty to Antoine, she told herself. Yet Stratford's face haunted her. And so did the thought of his monumental fury when he discovered what she had done.

Dark had fallen when the coach clattered under the huge sign of the Red Fox Inn and into its cobblestone courtyard. Diana resented the curious appraisal of the inn's proprietor, a short, fat man with gray hair that hung in clumps. She had hoped that Antoine might be there awaiting her arrival, but he was not. Nor was there any message from him. Not knowing what else to do, she took a room for herself where she could wait until he arrived.

The innkeeper was clearly suspicious of a woman whose coach bespoke respectability traveling alone without so much as an abigail in such rough country, where smugglers and pirates often sought refuge. He tried to draw her into conversation. But Diana brushed aside his questions, and he had had enough visitors on dubious errands to have learned long before not to press reluctant customers. Instead, he contented himself with charging her twice his usual rate.

Since Diana's purse was exceedingly thin, she blanched inwardly at the sum. But innocent of the avaricious ways of country innkeepers, she paid it.

The room that she was allotted was small but adequate. The bed was piled high with feather mattresses, and a set of steps had been placed beside it. To her relief, the linen was fresh and white, and the rooms were clean, although the carpets were a trifle threadbare.

Diana began pacing the tiny confines, nervously hoping that Antoine would soon appear, but he did not.

Finally, she heard the clatter of a coach in the courtyard, and her heart leaping with hope, she ran to the window. Looking down, she saw a portly man in a billowing gold redingote emerge from the vehicle. The light from the flaring torches in the courtyard illuminated his face. Diana recognized Lord Rudolph Oldfield, who was considered the nastiest gossip in all London. She groaned in annoyance.

More time passed, and Diana sank down in a wing chair. With each passing moment, she was becoming more certain that Antoine, the smugglers, and their ship had either been captured or sent to the bottom of the sea.

She ordered a light supper sent up to her room. In her haste to reach the inn, she had not stopped on the road for food. She had eaten nothing all day except a piece of bread and butter before she had left her father's house in London. Still, when the supper arrived, she was so distraught over what might have happened to Antoine and over her own precarious position that she could only nibble at the food.

She had not the slightest notion of what to do in the morning if Antoine had not arrived by then. She had not the money for another night at such an exorbitant inn, but where could she go? She knew no one in that part of the country upon whose charity she could throw herself. Her head had begun to ache fiercely. She released her long blond hair from its pins, letting it fall around her shoulders, and started brushing it vigorously to keep her nervous hands busy.

The minutes passed like hours. The candles guttered out one by one until only one stub remained lit. Diana's hope had sputtered out with the candles. Antoine would not come.

She sat numbly in the wing chair, unable to rouse herself from the despair into which she had sunk. She would have no choice on the morrow but to go back to London.

Yet what was she to do when she got there? She could not imagine that Stratford would marry her now. Nor was her father likely to allow her back in his house. Delighted by the excuse she had given him, Landane would turn her out without a penny, while her fortune would still be withheld from her because she was unmarried. What would she do?

She was too exhausted to think. She must try to get some sleep. If ever she needed all her wits, it was now. Wearily, she rose from the chair, opened her portmanteau, pulled out a blue lawn nightgown, and undressed.

She pulled on the thin night shift, tied its narrow blue satin ribbon that ran beneath her firm, full bosom, and climbed up the steps into the bed.

There she began to weep in despair. Even if she crawled on her knees to Stratford, he would never forgive her for her attempt to humiliate him before the world by eloping with another man. But it was more than fear of his anger that pained her. It was the knowledge of how shabbily she had treated him. And most painful of all was the knowledge that it was he whom she cared for, not Antoine. What a hideous mull she had made of things.

It was a long, long time before she fell into a restless, fitful sleep.

CHAPTER 17

George Whorton, a worried frown on his face, waited until Diana had left for her fittings in Bond Street, then departed himself from Landane's residence in Chesterfield Street. He went immediately to St. James, where he called upon the duke of Stratford, who had arisen but a few minutes before and received George in a brocade dressing gown. The two men were closeted for some time. After George left, the duke dressed more quickly than was his wont and soon drove off in his landau on an errand of his own. That completed, he drove on to his agent's office.

It was afternoon when he drove up to the couturier's establishment in Bond Street. He did not expect Diana to still be there, but he wished to make certain she had made no changes in what he had ordered for her. To his surprise, he found Landane's coach and coachman still waiting patiently in front of the shop.

Alarm flashed in the duke's mind, and a hasty foray into the shop confirmed his surmise. He rushed outside to accost the startled James.

"You fool, where did Miss Landane go?"

The befuddled James could only point toward the shop.

"Did you see her enter that shop?"

James shook his head slowly. "The miss, she sent me on."

Alexander swore and jumped back into his landau, heading at top speed for Landane's house. There he found Landane just returning home.

"Where is your daughter?" Stratford demanded, his eyes blazing.

"Here, I assume," Landane stammered, much disconcerted by the duke's anger.

But Diana was not there and had not been since morning.

Stratford's temper was not at all improved by the reaction of Mrs. Cottam, still abed with her nerves, to the news that her charge had disappeared. She promptly fainted, and a vinaigrette of smelling salts had to be found to revive her. The duke had no patience with women who fainted, and when Mrs. Cottam came to, he demanded roughly, "Where would Miss Landane have gone? Surely she told you something."

Mrs. Cottam clutched at the vinaigrette and appeared to be on the verge of fainting again at the duke's angry insinuation.

He grabbed her arms. "Don't you dare faint again. I haven't time for such nonsense now. Tell me where Miss Landane has gone."

Mrs. Cottam did not faint. Instead, she burst into tears. Between sobs she managed to get out that she had not the slightest idea where Diana might have gone, nor would she, Mrs. Cottam, have countenanced such a thing as Diana's running away.

Giving up in disgust, Stratford stalked from the room, followed by Landane. In the drawing room, the duke paced angrily as Landane nervously tried to mollify him. "Perhaps, Your Grace, she met with an accident," Landane said hopefully.

The duke gave him a withering glance. "An accident within the five feet between the coach and the door of the couturier's? Nonsense. She has run away. This is her revenge for my forcing her into a marriage not to her liking. She thinks she will humiliate me by showing the world she has jilted me." He slammed his right fist into the palm of his left hand with such a crack that Landane jumped. "But I shall outwit her." He whirled on Landane. "You are not to breathe a word of this."

"Of course not," Landane stammered nervously. "We—we must begin a search for her at once."

"And pray, in which direction are we to search?" the duke asked.

Landane's florid face was puzzled. After thinking for a moment, he suggested, "Greycote."

"Unfortunately, your daughter is not stupid. I do not know where she might go, but I am certain that would be the last place." He began pacing again. "Send for Stanley Pearce. He might have a clue. In the meantime, let us look in her room."

A servant was hastily dispatched for Mr. Pearce, and the duke stalked up to Diana's room. What he discovered there further alarmed him.

"Her glasses are still here," Landane exclaimed. "She would not leave without them. She is quite blind."

"She is no more blind than I am," Alexander snapped. He unscrewed the cap from one of the jars that cluttered the top of her dressing table and regarded its ugly yellow contents with disgust. "She left her eyeglasses here for the same reason she left these jars. She has no more need of her disguise."

His lordship stared at the duke as though he had lost his wits. "What are you talking about?"

Stratford gave Landane a pitying glance and was saved from having to answer by the appearance of a footman in the doorway.

"Your lordship," the footman said, "a messenger is downstairs with an urgent message for Miss Landane that he says he must personally deliver into her own hands and her hands alone."

Landane glared at the intruding servant. "Get rid of him."

"No." Alexander ordered curtly. "I shall handle it."

He went downstairs to the messenger, a mud-stained youth much out of breath after what had evidently been a long, hard ride.

Stratford noted that the messenger had a fresh cut across

his cheek and that his left arm was heavily bandaged. The duke gave the bedraggled youth his most persuasive smile. "Miss Landane is very ill abed, and the doctor has forbidden her all visitors. I fear I cannot permit you to disturb her. However, if you leave the message with me, I shall see that she gets it immediately."

The youth looked at him doubtfully, obviously confused by that piece of news. "But my master insisted I must see this into her hands only." He held up a letter. "I am to give it to no one else save her."

"I fear you shall have a long wait, then," Stratford said.

"But it can't wait," the youth cried. "'Tis most urgent. It was to have been delivered last night at the very latest, but I met with an accident upon the road and have been delayed."

"Then I shall take it up to her at once," Stratford said firmly, extracting the letter from the messenger's reluctant fingers. "Wait here in case she wishes to send an answer."

Stratford went back upstairs to Diana's room, where he broke open the seal. He glanced first at the salutation, "My most beloved Diana," and then at the signature, "All my love, Antoine." But it was what lay between that turned the duke's face to stone. He shoved the missive in his pocket and went back downstairs, where he told the messenger, "Miss Landane says she is too ill to answer now."

After the messenger had left, Stratford whirled on Landane. "You did not tell me your daughter had a lover."

Landane was genuinely shocked. "A lover? That's impossible. Who would—" He broke off, reddened, and stammered, "I mean . . ."

He was spared from having to explain what he might mean by the arrival of Mr. Pearce.

"Diana has run off to elope with Antoine," Stratford told the old man, then turned and stalked out the door and into the night.

Pearce watched him go, then shook his gray head sadly.

"What a pity. Stratford would have made her a good husband, but he will never marry her now."

"Not marry her?" Landane quivered. "But what will Isabel say? He must marry her."

"You fool," Pearce said contemptuously. "This is the worst insult the duke has ever been dealt. To finally choose a wife, only to have her run off almost on the eve of the wedding with a penniless Frenchman. Stratford will be the laughingstock of all England if it's known."

"What will he do? Where is he going?"

"I suspect to stop the elopement and bring her back here. He won't marry her, but he won't let her marry Antoine, either, if he can prevent it."

Returning to his house in St. James, the duke ordered his fastest horse saddled as he changed into his buckskin riding breeches and his tall boots, polished to such a sheen he could see his reflection in them. He stuffed a brace of pistols in his belt and was on his way, galloping through the cloudy night toward the coast. The look on his face was dreadful to behold.

CHAPTER 18

Diana was roused from her restless slumber in her bed at the Red Fox Inn by a hard pounding on her door. Antoine, she thought sleepily. She was so relieved that she jumped from the bed and, quite unmindful of her state of undress, ran to the door. "Antoine," she cried as she flung it open.

Stratford's hard face, his gray eyes blazing, stared back at her.

"No," she gasped. So great was her shock and horror that her legs would no longer support her. She would have sunk to the floor had he not caught her in his right arm and held her upright. In his left hand he held a lantern.

"Yes," he growled. He stepped inside, still holding her in his punishing grip, and kicked the door shut with his foot. He set the lantern down on a small table just inside the door and stared at her. Her hair tumbled over her bare shoulders and down about her upper body in a golden torrent. Eyes as blue as sapphires stared back at him in terror.

"So this is what the ugly Miss Landane really looks like." The gray eyes glittered mockingly. "When I said I wanted to see the real you tonight, I did not suspect how far I would have to travel to do so. What I find almost makes the trip worth it. I suspected you were pretty but not this lovely."

He stepped back so that he held her at arm's length, studying the lovely body revealed by the sheer, clinging night shift.

Her face flaming with embarrassment, Diana tried desperately to shield her body from his gaze with her hands.

He laughed harshly at her awkward efforts. "You have no compunction about greeting your lover half-naked. Pray, why your sudden modesty in front of your betrothed?"

He released his grip on her left arm, and his fingers toyed with a golden curl that hung over one breast. Then his hand slid possessively over it down to her waist and over her hip.

His touch set off a tremor of excitement in her. Shocked, she pulled away from him. Seeing the mockery in his eyes, she knew that he, too, had felt her response.

She snatched up her cloak, lying on a chair, and wrapped

its ample folds around herself. "Antoine is not my lover—yet." She spat out the last word defiantly, in retaliation for her own humiliation, and instantly regretted her foolishness when she saw Alexander's cheeks color with fury.

"You vixen. You allowed our betrothal to be announced and our bans to be published, knowing all the while that you planned to run off with Antoine. Why did you so want to humiliate me?"

"Because you were so arrogant, insufferable, and uncaring. You thought I should be delighted that you deigned to make me your wife when, in truth, you were just another fortune hunter."

"Less a fortune hunter than Antoine."

"That's a lie."

"Is it? Then why did he send you this letter?" The duke pulled from his coat pocket the letter that had been delivered by the mud-stained messenger and thrust it into her hands. "This came for you tonight. I took the liberty of opening it. That's how I found you."

She stared blankly at the paper in her hand, its red wax seal broken.

"Go ahead, read it. Then tell me your lover isn't a fortune hunter."

Slowly, she went to the table where the lantern flickered. She smoothed out the paper and moved the lantern closer to catch the weak light on the letter. She did not need to look at the signature to know that it had been written by Antoine. The curious back slant of the writing told her that.

The letter was a long one, filled with many flowery expressions of Antoine's undying love for her and encomiums to her beauty and brilliance so fulsome that they reeked of insincerity and nearly buried the real reason for the letter in their verbiage. Antoine wrote that a storm had delayed his sailing to England. Because of that and various other vague difficulties and complications, it would be impossible for him to reach England until two weeks after her wedding to the duke.

"You must go through with the wedding or we shall be lost," he wrote. "We dare not arouse suspicion. Otherwise, you will be so closely watched that we can never hope to escape. But do not fear. I shall rescue you from your dreaded union with the duke very quickly and carry you far from his reach. Do not chafe too much at marrying him, for it will be to our benefit. You will have fulfilled the stipulation in your grandfather's will, and his fortune will be yours."

Diana refolded the letter mechanically, her eyes blind with pain. Her heart, indeed her whole body, ached at his perfidiousness. She longed to throw herself upon the bed and sob out her grief and outrage, but her pride would not permit her to do so in front of the duke.

Alexander, his gray eyes hard, said coldly, "'Tis strange, is it not, that although a storm prevented him from reaching these shores, it did not prevent his servant from doing so with this letter."

She gave him a look of pure misery, and the tears she could no longer hold back glistened in her eyes. "You need point out nothing to me, my lord duke. I am not so stupid that I fail to realize from this letter that Antoine's only interest in me was my fortune. Just as it was your only interest." The tears trickled down her cheeks, and in a small, miserable voice she asked, more of herself than of the duke, "Did Antoine really think that once I was married, I would break my vows and flee with him?"

The duke snorted contemptuously. "You seem to perceive a difference between a vow to wed and the marriage vow itself."

Diana raised her tear-stained eyes to him. "Yes, I do perceive a difference. I made no vow to marry you. I was told I must and given no voice in the matter. But the other—it is binding before God. If I had married you, I should have been faithful to you."

"But you never intended to marry me. You pretended to go along with my offer merely to humiliate and hurt me."

She rose from the table and stood defiantly before him. "If it were your heart instead of merely your pride that would have been hurt, I should have been very sorry indeed. Since you are so concerned about feelings, my lord duke, think just once of how you hurt me." She saw him start. "Yes, hurt me," she repeated. "Did you court me? Did you try to win my affection? No, you thought I would be so grateful for your offer that you did not even grant me the courtesy of asking me. Instead, you told me in a voice dripping with arrogant condescension, 'I have decided to marry you,' as if your decision were all that could possibly matter. You were so contemptuous of my feelings that I was not consulted about the date or the location of my wedding, or even permitted to choose my gown and trousseau."

"You told me that first night at Greycote that you were not the least romantic." Alexander's gray eyes were strange and unfathomable. "Now I find you wanted romance, too."

"Not romance, my lord duke, but a husband who cared for me." A sob that she could not stifle broke in her throat. "Are you certain my income is large enough to keep Lady Bradwell in emeralds?"

The duke's right eyebrow arched quizzically. "I did not think you cared much for jewels."

"I don't," she said with another tiny sob. "That's not the point."

Stratford smiled sardonically. "Besides, emeralds would not suit you."

Stung, she glared at him. "Of course not. Emeralds would be too brilliant for such a poor creature as I." She brushed at the angry tears now staining her cheeks. "I will tell you what else does not suit me—a marriage of convenience to a loathsome man like you.''

The anger rekindled in his eyes, and he seized her arms. ''We both know I am not so loathsome to you as you pretend.''

''No,'' she gasped, jerking free of him. She fled to the door. Letting go of the cloak she was clutching around her, she tugged the door open. As the cloak fell to the floor, the duke grabbed her and wrapped her in his embrace, kissing her hard, his mouth sealing off her protest. He was far too strong for her to struggle against, and she was forced to accept his burning kiss, which to her chagrin was far from loathsome to her.

A shrill, unpleasant laugh rang out in the hallway, and a high-pitched voice said, '' 'Pon my word, Your Grace, you are getting very public about your amours.''

The duke's head jerked up from Diana's lips.

Lord Rudolph Oldfield was watching them from the hall, a lascivious smile spread across his face. ''A last-minute frolic before your nuptials, Your Grace?'' Oldfield's lecherous eyes appreciatively inspected Diana's body, scarcely concealed by the sheer night shift.

Her face burned crimson with embarrassment, and a humiliated moan rose in her throat. Alexander swore softly.

''What a fine morsel you have picked this time, Your Grace, but then your taste always was the best. I hear, though, that your future duchess is quite ugly. But her money is beautiful.''

Alexander snatched up the cloak from the floor and wrapped Diana in it. Then he held her close to him as though to protect her from Oldfield's leer. His body was stiff with anger against hers. ''I may kill you for the lies you have just uttered, Oldfield.''

The leer faded from Oldfield's face, and fear took its

place. The duke's hot temper and his dueling skills were too renowned to be taken lightly.

"This is my wife, Oldfield," the duke said in a dangerously quiet voice.

Diana gaped up at Alexander's stern, handsome face, wondering if he had gone quite mad.

"We were wed by special license this evening. Unless you apologize to her for your insults to her honor and her beauty, you shall accept my challenge to meet me on the field of honor at dawn."

The color faded from Oldfield's face, leaving it as pasty white as a loaf of unbaked bread about to be put in an oven.

"Well?" The duke's tone was ominous.

"Married—but I had no idea." Oldfield was shifting his heavy frame nervously from foot to foot. "Of course I apologize to your wife." He bowed deeply to Diana. "I beg you will forgive me. London gossip has done you an enormous injustice."

Alexander pulled Diana back from the door and said, "Now, Oldfield, if you will excuse us, we have matters of greater interest to attend to."

A knowing smile flickered on Oldfield's lips, but Alexander shut the door sharply on it, turning the key in the lock.

He turned to Diana. "Damn the luck. With all of England to choose from, did you have to pick for your elopement the inn where the most vicious gossip in London was staying."

"I did not write in advance asking for a list of my fellow guests," Diana shot back. "I am quite enlightened to learn I am a married woman."

"That Banbury tale will not prevent a scandal, but it will stop the worst of it."

"I would not think one more scandal involving a woman would matter much to you, my lord duke. You have been involved in so many of them."

"None of the women, however, was my duchess. The last thing on earth I want is a scandal involving my wife."

"I would be touched if your feeling sprang from solicitude for me instead of concern for your family's reputation. You seem to have forgotten one small point. I am not your wife, and when that gets out, the scandal will be all the greater."

"It will not get out." His face was set in the hard lines of a man determined to do his duty no matter how distasteful it was. "We will be married by dawn, and no one will ever be the wiser."

Diana's knees trembled, and she placed her hand on a chairback for support. "You cannot seriously intend to marry me now."

"I had not intended to, but I have no choice in the matter now, thanks to Oldfield."

"Oh, no," she gasped. She did not want to be married to a man who hated her and had wed her only out of duty. "Please, no."

He slammed his fist down hard on the table, causing the lantern to bounce precariously. "You little fool, you should be delighted that I am saving you from the consequences of your stupidity. If I do not marry you, you will be ruined. Your father will not take you back. Even if you could somehow convince him to, Isabel would see that he did not. What would you do then?"

Her head wobbled weakly from side to side as though her neck were no longer strong enough to support the burden. "I don't know," she whispered.

"Are you such a fool you still think your Antoine would take you?" the duke demanded harshly. "Especially when he learns that even if you are married, control of your fortune goes to your husband."

Diana wiped at her tears with a corner of the cloak. In her

pain she lashed out, "And what if you marry me? Aren't you afraid I might still run off with Antoine?"

She instantly regretted her taunt. Alexander's face was so furious that she shrank back from him.

"Perhaps you deserve him and the kind of life you would live with him," he ground out. "No doubt he would abandon you as soon as he found that your money was still beyond his reach, just as he abandoned his wife when he had gone through her fortune."

"What?"

Alexander repeated what Mr. Pearce had told him about Antoine.

Diana sank into the chair. "And to think that he was the only man other than George Whorton whom I ever for a moment trusted," she cried in a voice choked with loathing and disillusionment. She stared blankly down at the floor, tears trickling down her cheeks.

Alexander said nothing, only watched her.

In an anguished whisper, she asked, more of herself than of him, "Was it so much to want a husband who would cherish me, who would be both lover and companion, want me, not just want my fortune?"

Alexander's gray eyes studied her with a strange intensity. His face was a mask. Finally, he said quietly, "I made a horrible mistake with you, Diana." He broke off, making a gesture of futility with his hands. "Oh, to hell with it. It is too late now. We must be married at once. We have no choice." He went to the door. "Get dressed while I have your horses harnessed. We will leave in a quarter hour."

As Alexander led Diana down the stairway of the Red Fox Inn, she complained, "It will be well into the morning before we reach London."

"We are not going to London. We are going to Mistelay."

"Mistelay!" she cried as they stepped into the cobble-stone courtyard. "But you cannot take me there when we are not married."

"It is a trifle late to be worrying about your reputation," he said dryly.

Tebbets was standing by the coach, his face a woebegotten blend of fright and misery. As Stratford handed her into the vehicle, Tebbets hung his head and refused to meet her gaze. Diana wondered what Stratford had said to the poor man to make him cower as he did.

To her relief, the duke did not join her in the coach but elected to ride on a horse hired from the inn's stable, his own having been worn out by the long trip from London. Once out of sight of the inn, the duke ordered Tebbets to push the horses forward at top speed. Stratford himself rode on ahead, and his horse's hoofbeats soon faded in the distance.

As the vehicle jolted along, Diana sank back on the brown leather cushions, her mind and her heart in turmoil. The pain that gnawed at her heart had less to do with Antoine, whom she now detested, than with Alexander. In light of Stratford's kindness, courtesy, and consideration to her upon her arrival in London, there might have been hope for an acceptable accommodation in their marriage had she made a similar effort instead of sinking herself beneath reproach by trying to elope with Antoine. If only she had listened to George Whorton. If only she had abandoned her foolish scheme of escape.

She remembered with shriveling heart Alexander's bitter statement that he had made a horrible mistake with her. The mistake, of course, had been his blurting out in anger to Oldfield that they were already wed. Now he was trapped into a marriage he no longer wished. How bitterly he must be cursing his tongue—as well as her.

The low, hoarse croak of a night heron in the distance

interrupted her painful thoughts. She wondered how much longer it would be before she reached Mistelay, with its great house and famous gardens. Her marriage might be made in hell, but at least its setting would be heavenly.

It was past three A.M. when the coach rumbled up the winding driveway that led to the mansion entrance. Thick clouds cloaked both moon and stars in inky darkness broken only by the coach's lanterns, the merest pinpricks of light in the vast blackness that cloaked the earth. She could see nothing of the grounds but the broad outlines of great evergreens, towering like giant sentinels in the dark. The palace, too, was so concealed by the black night that Diana could scarcely make out the great pillared portico as they drove up. A blazing torch in an iron holder illuminated the entrance.

The duke himself opened the great oak doors for her, and she stepped into a hall that was large and empty of furniture, art, even servants. It had a cold, forbidding air that cast additional gloom on her already-depressed spirits.

Alexander, standing alone in the hall, had changed from his travel-stained buckskins and muddy boots into white silk pantaloons, satin waistcoat, and a blue velvet jacket. His hair had been brushed neatly about his face, and he was newly shaven. At first glance, he looked remarkably fresh for a man who had spent most of the night in the saddle, but a closer scrutiny revealed tiny lines of weariness carved deeply about his eyes and mouth. Still, he looked as elegant as though he were setting out for an evening at court, making Diana feel all the more bedraggled in her old cloak and wrinkled gown.

He plucked the cloak from her shoulders, saying in a quiet, emotionless voice, "The Reverend Gibson is waiting in the chapel to marry us."

"Now?" Diana gasped.

"Now. After your folly, the quicker we are wed, the better. By tonight Oldfield will have broadcast to all London that we are married." A touch of sarcastic humor seasoned Alexander's voice. "It would never do to make that malicious old gossip a liar, now would it?"

She gestured down at her travel-wrinkled dress of striped pink-and-cream silk. "At least let me change my clothes and repair myself."

Alexander's right eyebrow rose in a high arch. "I think not. Your gown is a trifle travel worn, but still it is by far the most attractive I have yet been permitted to see you in. And heaven knows what damage you might do to that lovely face of yours should I let you loose among those pots of yours." He took her arm. "Come, we are keeping the Reverend Gibson waiting."

"We have no license," she protested.

He pulled a document from his coat pocket. "But we do, thanks to George Whorton's unease."

"So even George has betrayed me," Diana said bitterly. "Is there no man who can be trusted?"

"George wanted to help, not hurt you. He had your best interests at heart. After his warning, I took the precaution of obtaining a special license in the event you might do something foolish." His mouth tightened. "Neither of us dreamed, however, that you would attempt such treachery as you did."

CHAPTER 19

The sun was already nearing its zenith when Diana awoke the next morning in her bedchamber in the ducal apartments. For a moment, as she gazed up at the worn fringed bed hangings, she was uncertain where she was. Then the memory of the dreadful night before engulfed her like a bad dream.

She was now the duchess of Stratford, at least in name. What an odd wedding it had been in the tiny chapel that Alexander's pious great-grandmother—or had it been his great-great-grandmother—had installed at Mistelay. Only two tall tapers on the altar had challenged the darkness of the tiny room.

The Reverend Gibson, a thin, jumpy man, so obsequious to the duke that it had sickened Diana, had been more nervous than either the bride or groom. He had scarcely been able to get the words of the ceremony out. It had taken no more than five minutes. As soon as Gibson had pronounced her and Alexander man and wife, her groom had not even stopped to kiss her before hurrying the minister out.

Then her new husband, his face harsh in the shadowy light, led her silently up the stairs to the ducal apartments, where he had opened the door to her chamber and stepped back to allow her to enter.

"This is your room," he told Diana. "There are no servants about, so you will have to manage for yourself." He turned on his heel and vanished into the adjoining room without so much as saying good night, much less kissing her. She was left to spend her wedding night alone. As she lay unloved and miserable in her bed, she heard Alexander's restless pacing in the next room, prompted no doubt by his distress at having had to marry her at all.

Now, as she examined her bedchamber in the light of day,

it seemed even shabbier than it had in the candlelight of the night. It was sparsely furnished with only a bed, an oak Farthingale chair, and a carved oak cupboard. The bed was also of carved oak, heavy and much battered, as were the other pieces of furniture. They looked like shabby rejects rescued from a storage room to which they had been consigned decades before. The draperies, like the bed hangings, were threadbare and faded. Only the ceiling of the large chamber, with its elaborate scrollwork, and the handsome white marble chimneypiece inlaid with ivy of green-and-brown marble were of the quality that she would have expected to find at the great Mistelay.

Slowly, she dressed, not knowing what to do or what was expected of her. Perhaps a walk in the famous gardens would raise her spirits, so depressed by the ominous start of her marriage.

Diana hurried down the broad marble staircase with its ornate balustrade, praying that she would not meet her husband on the stairs. In her present sunken spirits she did not feel able to face him.

In the great hall, which appeared even larger and emptier in the daylight than it had the night before, Diana met a tall, bony woman with a thin face as gray as her hair. "Your Grace." The woman gave an awkward courtesy. "Mrs. Gill here." Seeing the blank look on Diana's face, she explained, "Me and the mister is the caretakers."

Mrs. Gill quickly launched into a long and disjointed apology for the state of Mistelay, explaining that the duke had not so much as set foot in the place these past months and even after his betrothal had given no orders to prepare the house for his bride's homecoming. Then he had appeared without warning in the early hours of that very morning, giving them but a half-hour's notice of her arrival.

"He mighta given us more warning, he mighta," Mrs. Bill complained. "Scared me half out of me wits, he did, when he came agalloping up in the middle of the night like that. The mister and me, we thought it be the burglars again.'' The woman gave Diana a side glance that was filled with curiosity. "I says to the mister, I says, 'What will His Grace's poor bride be athinking of us—what with the place alooking like a jungle and the house almost as bare as His Grace himself was the day he was born.' "

Diana managed to suppress her amusement as the woman stopped for breath, then plunged on. "And no servants, neither. Let all the staff but the mister and me go long ago, His Grace did. Even fired all the gardeners; not what they didn't deserve it. Never seen such a crowd of lazy louts. Scarcely did a lick of work after the old head gardener, Staines, died.''

Mrs. Gill paused, and her mind rambled back to the present. "I says to the mister, I says, 'What will the poor new duchess be athinking when she finds not even a chambermaid to lay a proper fire in her room or a cook to dress a proper meal for her?' '' Mrs. Gill was clearly scandalized by His Grace's careless introduction of his bride to Mistelay. "And you not even having your maid with you. I offered to stay up to help when you arrived, but His Grace wouldn't hear of it. Ordered me and the mister back to bed, he did. It's not like His Grace to be so inconsiderate. I says to the mister, I says, 'If his mama were here, she'd've given him a good tongue-lashing, she'd've, for such inconsideration.' And the duke, he'd alistened, too. The old duchess, she had a blunt tongue, she did, and when she spoke, he listened.''

"They must have gotten along poorly."

Diana's observation astonished Mrs. Gill. "Not got along with her! Why, he adored her. Like bread and butter, they was. Never was a son kinder to his mama. 'Twas after her death that he stopped acoming here. It was too lonely with her gone. She was a lively one, she was.'' Mrs. Gill pursed her lips into a disapproving little ring. "But that don't ex-cuse him none for the way he's let Mistelay go and been selling off its furnishings. Why, I says to the mister only the other day, I says, 'At the rate it's going, the grounds'll be a jungle, and the house'll be empty in another year.'"

Diana looked around the hall. So that was why it was so bare. She had not dreamed that Stratford was in quite such dreadful financial straits that he had been reduced to selling off the furnishings of his ancestral home. No wonder he had been so determined to marry her. He was so desperate that he had been forced to overlook her lack of beauty, her antip-athy to the match, and even her effort to flee with another man. He could not afford to let her fortune escape him. A man as proud as he would hate her for trying to spurn him, but a man as proud as he would prefer a hated marriage to acknowledging to the world that he was financially ruined.

Sick at heart, Diana managed to escape Mrs. Gill and went out to inspect firsthand the ruin into which the grounds had fallen. The day was sunny but with a crispness that nipped at her cheeks. A dismal sight lay before her. Al-though the snow had melted, the green of spring had not yet vanquished the brown pallor of winter on the overgrown lawns, where an army of weeds was now encamped.

The gardens, when Diana reached them, were even more disappointing. What had once been order was now chaos. Untamed yew and box hedges were growing wild and scrag-gly, encroaching on the paths. Flower beds lay barren or choked with weeds and dead remains. Long-untended topi-aries had taken on grotesquely misshapen forms, and ivy rampaging out of control threatened to overrun everything.

She continued on at a brisk pace, gripped by dismay as she regarded the neglected tangle that once had been legend-ary gardens.

She entered the woods and quickly found the path impass-able. Dreadful thickets and bushes, some with cruel thorns, others wild offspring of windborne seed, tore at her. There, too, ivy was growing rampantly, sending out its long, looping tendrils to embrace the slender trunks of young Norway maples.

She turned back toward the house, her depression deepened by the neglect that surrounded her. It would take an army of gardeners to hack away the cancerous growth of negligence and restore the grounds to their former beauty. She brushed against a leafless branch of a goat willow and reached up to pull off one of its fluffy yellow catkins.

Diana walked along an out-of-control box hedge as high as her shoulders, staring down thoughtfully at the yellow catkin in her hand. Would she be as neglected by Stratford as his house and grounds were? Obviously he cared for neither. Would he exile her there with his other rejected possessions? And if he did, what could she do about it? She had inflicted a most painful wound on his pride, and she doubted he would ever forgive her. Yet if her life was to be bearable, she must somehow find a way to make their marriage one of mutual toleration, although it could never be one of love. Not now.

"I'm pleased to see that you are returning to the house." Her husband's voice very near her made her jump.

Looking up, Diana saw that he was on the other side of the tall hedge. It concealed all but his face. Despite herself, her heart beat faster at the sight of him. She was relieved to see that the harsh, angry lines of the previous night had relaxed, and he appeared to be in good humor. How handsome he looked. It was so painful to be married to such a man when she knew she could never capture his heart.

"Surely you were not afraid that I was running away," she said sweetly, carefully hiding her distress.

"I am persuaded, my dear wife, that you would do anything to embarrass me."

"Such persuasions must be the price you pay for marrying a woman you do not love."

"How can I love you when you do naught but insult me and try to drive me away?" Stratford fell into step with her, and they walked along, separated by the high hedge. "Have you been weeping inconsolably for your lost lover?"

His cool, careless tone stung her already-exacerbated emotions, and she snapped, "He was not worth wasting my tears on. I count my blessings to be rid of him. If only I could say the same of you, my lord duke, my happiness would be complete."

Now he, too, was angry. "Stop calling me my lord duke. My name is Alex."

Diana recalled when her father had made the mistake of calling the duke Alex. "You made quite a point of telling my father that your name is Alexander."

He laughed. "But you may call me Alex."

"So I am among the privileged few," she retorted angrily.

"You are the most privileged of all," he teased, smiling across the hedge at her. "You are my wife."

The smile and the softness of his voice sent a quiver through her. Still, she could not stop her evil tongue from retorting, "I am sorry, my lord duke. I do not consider that a privilege but a calamity."

"Diana," he said quietly, "we are married now, and we might as well make the best of it. We accomplish nothing by ripping at each other."

His sudden quiet forbearance in the face of her churlishness shamed her. And his desire to make the best of their marriage heartened her. "You are right, my lor—Alexander. I am sorry."

He smiled. "At least that's better than my lord duke."

They reached a gap in the hedge, and he stepped through

it to join her. She was surprised to see that he was carrying a straw basket filled with daffodils and wild violets.

"How lovely!" she exclaimed. "What are the flowers for?"

"You." He handed her the basket. "I know how much you like them. Mistelay's greenhouses, like everything else here, have fallen into decay and ruin. So until they are repaired, you will have to make do with the wild variety."

As she took the basket, she saw that he was watching her with an anxious expression, like that of a child waiting to see if his gift meets with approval. Touched, she reached out with her free hand and brushed his arm. "Thank you."

They walked across the weed-choked lawn toward the Palladian mansion, with its pillared and pedimented portico, which reminded Diana of a Roman temple.

"What do you think of your new home?" he asked her. "Honestly."

"Honestly, I am shocked by how sad a state it is in."

Pain flashed in the gray eyes. "And you have seen only a little of the house. You will find the rest even more distressing."

He was right. As he led her through the barren rooms, stripped of furnishings and art, she grew more and more appalled.

In the great saloon, the long table that had seated fifty comfortably for dinner was gone. So were its chairs. The glass-enclosed cabinets along the walls that once had contained noted collections of Sevres, Meissen, and Chinese porcelains were empty. The only decoration now in the vast, empty hall was twenty feet overhead, a ceiling painstakingly decorated with intricately carved plaster scrollwork and inset with murals.

Relief surged through Diana when she entered the library. It had escaped the fate of the other rooms and, with its carved oak paneling, had an inviting warmth to it. Built-in bookcases containing hundreds of leather-bound volumes, their titles stamped in gold, lined three sides of the room. The fourth wall had long mullioned windows that looked out on an overgrown garden and a serpentine much clogged with moss and debris. Diana, who had railed at the limited library at Greycote, ached to study the book titles, but she restrained herself and followed her husband upstairs.

Alexander's bedchamber surprised her the most. It was dominated by a huge, grotesquely carved bed. Massive, heavily carved oak pillars supported an oak canopy. The Stratford coat of arms was carved in high relief on the headboard. The entire room from walls to windows and bed was hung with sadly worn velvet that once might have been blue but had faded to a dingy gray.

Like the bed, the other furnishings were also bulky remnants of the Stuart age—an oak cupboard with paneled door, its upper frieze carved with rosettes, an oak chest with diamond and lunette carvings on its panels, an oak table, a carved armchair.

"It's so gloomy," Diana protested.

"Yes, isn't it dreadful?" Alexander looked around with distaste.

"Why don't you change it?"

"The furnishings were originally installed by the third duke and have been here ever since. My father considered everything here a tradition he was bound to maintain, and he did so. After he died in this room, my mother asked that it be kept just as it was. Naturally, I granted her request."

"Even though you hated it?"

"It was her wish," he replied simply.

The arrogant duke as dutiful and loving son was an image that until very recently would have been beyond Diana's comprehension. But she had begun to regard her husband with altered eyes.

"But your mother is dead now."

Alexander nodded. "Since her death I have not come here at all. And the money it would have taken to redo the room was better applied to more pressing needs elsewhere."

"To Lady Bradwell's emeralds, for instance?"

"Those accursed emeralds seem to obsess you. Take a good look at this room. It is what Greycote will look like if Isabel has her way."

"You have neglected to show me the long gallery. It is Mistelay's most famous room."

"I was hoping you had not heard of it." With reluctant step, he led her downstairs. The gallery lived up to its name, being at least one hundred feet long. It was more on the scale of a cathedral than a gallery, Diana thought as she stared at the vast chamber with its intricately vaulted ceiling thirty feet above the polished parquet floor. Daylight filtered through the leaded casement windows. It looked even more vast than it was, because it contained not a single piece of furniture or work of art. All that remained of the renowned collection that had once been displayed there were the faint outlines on the walls marking where their frames had been. Even the portraits of the duke's predecessors were gone.

Diana was horror-struck, and even a little sick. How could Alexander have dissipated his heritage—and that of his descendants—in such a reckless and spendthrift fashion?

"You might at least have kept the portraits of your predecessors," she chided him.

Alexander stared out at the bedraggled gardens, pain etched on his face. "I could not bear for them to gaze down on their despoiled home."

"You have sold everything, haven't you?" She gestured angrily at the empty walls where once masterpieces had hung. "The furniture, the great paintings, the bronzes, the porcelain, everything."

"Not quite. The better art is packed away for safekeeping."

"How could you destroy your birthright like this? Tell me how many Rembrandts, and Van Dykes Lady Bradwell cost you."

Her angry question seemed to amuse him. "My, what a jealous shrew you are, my duchess."

His mocking tone raised her hackles. "I only regret that Lady Bradwell did not manage to effect a more permanent possession of you, my lord duke."

"'Tis comforting to know how dear I am to you."

"As dear as I am to you."

A strange smile played on his lips. "But my duchess, you are rather more dear to me than you think."

"You mean my fortune is."

"That, too. Behold my wedding present to you: Mistelay—to restore to its former glory."

"How generous of you," she commented bitterly.

He said mockingly, "I would have thought you would prefer the money be spent for this rather than for my mistresses. It is you who will live here and your son who will inherit it."

She turned hastily away from him so that he could not see the tears forming in her eyes. "Oh, yes, I nearly forgot my other use as your wife—to breed your heir." She did her best to sound defiant, but she could not hide her hurt.

Behind her, Alexander laid his hands on her arms with a gentleness that surprised her. She trembled at his unexpected touch, finding it most unsettling. "I expect more than that from you, my duchess. Besides, I thought you loved children and would welcome motherhood."

"I long for children, but you will not like how I view motherhood." She turned to face him, blue eyes full of determination. "I will not abandon them to be raised by nurses and nannies while I am off partying elsewhere. I know such views are definitely déclassé in the circles in which you move, but their mother will not be a stranger to her children even if their father is!''

To her surprise he did not seem displeased. Instead, he grinned broadly. ''What makes you think I should be a stranger to my children?''

''I am persuaded, my lord duke, that they would bore you infinitely.''

The haughty right eyebrow arched. ''Indeed? Did I seem bored with Amy Hill?'' Amusement danced in the gray eyes. ''It pains me to have to so grievously disillusion my duchess, but children delight me, and I look forward with enormous anticipation to having my own to romp with.''

She stared at him, not quite certain that she had heard him correctly. ''Really?''

''Really,'' he assured her. ''Now I would like you to start thinking about what you will do to Mistelay.''

''But why do you care about it? You never come here anymore.''

''Not now. Can you blame me when you see what I have been forced to let it become?'' Great sadness had replaced the laughter in his gray eyes. ''How I used to love to come here, especially in May, when the rhododendrons are in bloom. From May to September it was especially lovely here—once.''

Diana blurted out in surprise, ''Why, you care deeply about Mistelay, don't you?''

''More than you can guess.'' His answer was scarcely above a whisper.

Diana was suddenly very nervous about what he expected of her. ''What if you do not like what I do to Mistelay?''

''If you could turn that wretched pile of stone Greycote into what you did, I have high hopes for Mistelay.''

She was startled and pleased by the unexpected compliment—and by all she was learning about her complex husband. How little she understood him. She was astounded at how determined he seemed to make the best of their marriage. She had expected him to treat her with cold hostility that day. Instead, it had been only her own uncontrollable tongue that had seemed bent on keeping discord alive.

Diana eagerly began planning what she would do to Mistelay. She loved decorating, and she felt like a child turned loose in a mansion filled with toys. She made sketches of what she envisioned and lists of what she would need. She so frequently sought Alexander's opinion on what he would prefer that she began to fear she was becoming a nuisance. But he seemed to enjoy her enthusiasm and assured her that she was not bothering him.

But there remained one enormous blot on her happiness. Although Alexander was unfailingly cordial and considerate to her, he made no effort to make her fully his wife. Each night he escorted her to the door of her bedchamber and left her there. She was too hurt and humiliated by this nocturnal abandonment to ask him the reason. She could only guess that having so long enjoyed the great and notorious beauties of the age, he must find her less than exciting. Five days after their arrival, Alexander announced that they were returning to London on the morrow.

Diana was dismayed. "But I have so much to do here."

"By now you have a good idea of what you need, and you will be able to look for it in London."

She was struck by a sudden premonition, as vague as it was powerful, that London would mean disaster for her marriage. "I don't want to go."

"I am afraid I must insist that you do." His voice was soft, but it had that note of steel in it that told Diana it would be fruitless to oppose him.

She thought of the balls and dinners that she would have to attend with everyone staring at her. They would be whispering about the mysterious circumstances of her marriage and speculating whether the duke had married her only for her money. She turned beseeching eyes to him. "Please don't make me go there. I hate London society—people paying you compliments to your face and making fun of you behind your back."

He seized her hands in his own and squeezed them reassuringly. "Ninnyhammer," he said lightly, "you are much too sensitive. Besides, it will be different now. You are my wife."

"That will make it all the worse." She did not try to withdraw her hands from his, finding comfort in their warm clasp. "I can hear Lady Chattingham now." In a shrill, cracking voice that was an excellent imitation of the elderly harpy who was the vicious-tongued arbitrator of high society, Diana intoned, "What could Stratford possibly have seen in that antidote? Nothing but a country bumpkin—no wit, nor style, and so very long in the tooth. She has nothing, absolutely nothing, to recommend her except, of course, her fortune, and that is a very large recommendation."

Alexander gave a whoop of laughter. "Your imitation is perfect. If I closed my eyes, I would swear it was she talking." His handsome face turned serious. "However, you were wrong in almost every particular you gave of yourself. You are most assuredly neither an antidote nor a country bumpkin."

"But definitely long in the tooth."

"Not nearly so long as I."

"Oh, Alexander," she said miserably, "we are surely the talk of London. How do you expect to explain away our sudden marriage?"

"When you came up to London and I saw you again, I could not wait another day to make you my own." He twisted his face into a caricature of a lovesick swain. "I persuaded you to run off and marry me privately."

Diana laughed despite herself. "And I am persuaded that

even so polished a tongue as yours will have difficulty getting anyone to swallow that.''

He clasped her hands more tightly. ''I promise you, Diana, I will see to it that you do not find London hateful. Nor will you be the butt of that kind of vicious gossip.'' He removed one of his hands from hers and brushed her cheek gently. ''Trust me,'' he said softly. ''For once, trust me.''

CHAPTER 20

The duke of Stratford's first appearance in London society with his new duchess was to be the night after their return to town. Alexander selected the gown of blue satin that he wished Diana to wear to the affair, a ball given by the marquess of Tavenshire. The low bodice was embroidered with pearls and other brilliants, the color exactly matched her eyes, and the style enhanced the slender, soft curves of her body.

Before the hairdresser that Alexander had summoned for Diana was permitted to touch her long blond hair, he was given lengthy instructions by the duke on exactly how it was to be done. Diana watched in fascination as the hairdresser constructed her hair into an elaborate style piled high with curls that accentuated the delicate loveliness of her face. As she took a final glance at herself before joining Alexander, she thought that she had never looked so fine.

Her husband was, as usual, splendid in a coat of silk damask. Floral appliqués of silk crépe decorated the front, the tails, the pockets and cuffs. His breeches and stockings were white, and he wore japanned dress pumps with morocco heels.

As he took her arm to lead her down the stairs to their waiting carriage, he said, "You are so lovely tonight, my duchess. I am very proud to be your husband." He smiled down at her tenderly. Then they were at the carriage steps.

By the time they reached the marquess's, Diana was trembling with nervousness. No longer would she be plain Miss Landane who could hide unnoticed in a corner. That night she was the duchess of Stratford whose hasty marriage was the talk of the town. Every pair of eyes at the ball would be studying her, not only because of the peculiar circumstances of her marriage but out of curiosity over the woman the elusive Stratford had finally made his duchess.

As they entered the mansion, Alexander's arm firmly encircled her waist, and his reassuring voice whispered in her ear, "Don't worry. I promise you everything will go well. Trust me."

Because of him, it did go well. He stayed at her side throughout the evening, guiding the conversation, protecting her from any possible embarrassment, giving her confidence, and amusing her with a stream of witty comments and anecdotes about their fellow guests, until, to her amazement, she relaxed and actually began to enjoy herself.

From that night on, the social whirl in which she found herself never stopped. There was not a night at home, and even then Alexander rejected a dozen or more invitations for each one he accepted.

How successful Alexander was in dampening the scandalous rumors about their marriage was revealed to Diana one night at a rout when she chanced to overhear that notorious gossip Lady Lloyd tell her companion, "Of course I thought like everyone else that Stratford married that girl for her money. I was certain that story of his being in such a mad passion for her that he could not wait another day to marry her was a Banbury tale. But now, seeing the way he acts toward her, I am inclined to believe it.''

A wry smile twitched at Diana's lips. So great was Alexander's mad passion for her that their marriage was still unconsummated. Nevertheless, as Diana moved away, she took some consolation in the knowledge that at least the world thought Alexander loved her.

Diana quickly discovered that being Stratford's wife had enormous advantages. Not only did it convey upon her instant acceptance by the most lofty members of society, but she was treated with enormous deference and listened to with respect.

As the days passed, Diana actually came to enjoy the balls and dinners and assemblies that she had once so dreaded. Her pleasure stemmed in large measure from the fact that she shared a lively sense of the ridiculous with Alexander. Frequently, at an inane remark or ludicrous opinion she would look up and catch her husband's equally amused eye. Riding home in the carriage afterward, they would exchange lively impressions that left them both shaking with laughter. She was fascinated to discover, however, that Alexander's wicked tongue wounded only the fatuous, the priggish, and the foolish, of which London society furnished him a large assortment. He never turned his wit against those who could not help their failings. Her husband was kinder than she had thought.

Alexander quickly decided that Diana needed a larger wardrobe than he had initially ordered and selected additional gowns for her.

''I still prefer to choose my own clothes,'' she told him.

He flashed her an irresistible smile. ''I leave Mistelay in your hands, my duchess, but I shall insist upon the privilege of dressing you.'' His right eyebrow arched provocatively. ''I am reputed to have excellent taste in such matters.''

"And much practice," she retorted.

His gray eyes were teasing. "True, but no one has ever complained of my choices."

Nor when they arrived did Diana. Alexander's eye for what would look best on her was so unerring that she was delighted with his selections.

Not all of their nights were spent at balls and dinners. Alexander took her to Covent Garden and Drury Lane to see the plays and to a small house tucked away in Mayfair where Arthur Dowman, a writer and artist, presided over a salon of leading artists and literary figures. There the conversation turned upon philosophy and political issues, upon the respective merits of artists and writers, and it reminded Diana as nothing else in England ever had of Tante Germaine's brilliant gatherings at the villa on Lake Geneva. Diana would never have imagined that the duke of Stratford, with all his consequence, would be part of a circle like Dowman's, but it was apparent that he had long been a regular at the Mayfair house.

Diana's days were as busy as her evenings—what with searching London shops for materials for Mistelay, welcoming a steady stream of callers, and training the staff of Stratford's London house to her own exacting standards. She was determined to make it the best-run house in all the city.

Thus, three weeks passed swiftly. Alexander was all courtesy, affability, and generosity to her, in public and in private. Had they not already been married, one might have thought he was courting her. As the days passed, she found herself more and more captured by the spell of Alexander's charm. He could be irresistible when he set his mind to it. Never had she enjoyed anyone's company so much or felt such an overwhelming attraction for him.

Finally, she had to acknowledge to herself that she was wildly in love with her husband. That was, however, a source of pain, not happiness, to her, for despite Alexander's attention to her, he still gave no sign of wishing to make her his wife in more than name. Each night after they returned home from their round of parties, she would lie alone in her bed, hoping he would come to her. But he did not.

It was dreadful enough knowing that her husband, whom she loved, would never reciprocate her love, but it was unbearable that he found her so undesirable that even his wish for children did not bring him to her bed. Her pride would not permit her to discuss his reluctance to consummate their marriage.

His own bedchamber held a mystery—a locked room lay off it. When she had asked Alexander, he had been mysterious. He had fobbed her off by saying with teasing eyes that one of these days, if she did not plague him about it, he might show her what was in it.

Frequently, he was gone much of the day, saying only that he had business to attend to. Diana was haunted by the fear that the business was Lady Bradwell. The thought of the emerald necklace Alexander had so recently given her ladyship was enough to turn Diana the color of those precious stones.

Not that Diana could complain about her husband's generosity to her, for he was constantly giving her gifts, some as small as a Battesea box, others as large as a pair of grays for a canter in the park. So lavish was he to her that Mr. Pearce, paying her a visit one day, remarked that she had been quite justified in her fear that the duke would squander her money on a female. "But I hardly see that you can object, since that female is you," he said tartly.

Her favorite gift from Alexander remained the bust of Portia. She had had the bust of Hamlet brought up to London from Greycote, and now her two prized marbles resided in places of honor in the drawing room.

One night when the Stratfords had been but two hours at a party of Viscount Joynes, Alexander complained that the rooms were much overheated and suggested that they leave. Diana was quick to agree on both counts. The heat had caused her to sip more frequently than she should have from her glass of champagne, and now she was feeling a trifle giddy.

As they were riding home, their coach swerved suddenly to avoid an oncoming curricle, hurtling Diana roughly against her husband, who caught her. Bracing himself, he held her in his arms to prevent her from being further thrown about. She found herself clinging to him long after the need to do so had vanished. The champagne had made her languid, and she was so contented within the protection of his arm that she thought dreamily she would like to stay there forever.

Looking down at her, Alexander's right eyebrow raised in a quizzical arch, but he said nothing. Nor did he remove his arm. When several minutes had passed without her making any effort to move, he reached up with his free arm, turned her face toward his, and stroked her cheek softly with his fingertips. Then he bent his lips to hers and lightly brushed them. She returned his kiss with an intensity that astonished them both.

He wrapped his arms about her, and now his lips were demanding, parting hers, seeking the sweetness of her mouth. His kisses aroused such burning emotions in her that she was dismayed when the coach pulled to a stop in front of Stratford House. She wanted that wonderful moment to go on forever.

Her husband helped her down from the carriage and then, as was his wont, escorted her up the stairs to her bedchamber. Instead of leaving her at the door, however, he followed her in, saying, ''Don't bother to call your abigail. I make an excellent maid." As he spoke, he lifted her cloak from her shoulders and let it drop carelessly upon a chair.

"But not a very neat one," she retorted, her heart beating rapidly and her mouth dry with nervousness.

His lips closed over hers again, and his hands caressed her body, moving down her back and over her hips, molding her to him. The hard strength of his muscled body against hers excited her. She met his lips hungrily, her doubts of him and her inhibitions retarded by the lingering effects of the champagne. Suddenly, her gown fell from her shoulders, and she gasped as his quick fingers attacked the tiny buttons of her chemise. She tried to pull away from him, her face flaming.

"I am your husband," he reminded her pointedly, and quickly enveloped her in the warmth and reassurance of his embrace. Still she trembled, and he murmured comfortingly, unintelligibly, his breath warm upon her ear. His lips again sought hers, then moved down to her neck. His hand slipped beneath the thin batiste of her chemise and gently cupped her breast. His lips moved downward. His hands seemed everywhere, stroking the embers of her desire into her first flaming passion.

When he laid her on the bed, there was nothing hurried or harsh in his lovemaking. He was slow and tender, patiently awakening her uninitiated body to the rewards of love. Pain gave way to pleasure, fear to eagerness, ignorance to rapture, until she reached such heights that she did not think she could bear it.

When at last, near dawn, they lay exhausted, she snuggled against him, delighting in the feel of his warm body against hers. The first gray streaks of the new day were beginning to invade the room. Alexander's hair, damp from his exertion, curled about his face, and a dark stubble had appeared on his chin. There was no mistaking the gleam of triumph that was in his eyes and reflected in his face. "So you no longer find me so repulsive."

Although his voice was light and teasing, his words, coupled with that look, cut her like a knife. She flinched and drew back, but with a confident gesture of possession, he pulled her back to him and closed his eyes in sleep. The triumph still lingered on his face. It reminded her of that awful day at Greycote when he had announced his intention to marry her and then had kissed her to prove he could pleasure her should it be his own pleasure.

Sleep did not come to her as easily as it did to her husband. She was tormented by the question of whether his only intention had been to prove once again to her how easily he could make her want him, to prove to her that she was no different in that respect from all the others in his long line of conquests.

CHAPTER 21

When Diana awoke the next morning, Alexander had disappeared from her bed and the morning from her day. Her husband had gone out while she was still asleep, but neither his secretary nor his valet knew where. Diana could not decide whether she was pleased or unhappy over his absence. She was much troubled by his final, triumphant remark to her. He had conquered her heart as she had thought no man ever could, but she had not touched his. It was she, after all, who had started the previous night's events by clinging boldly to him in the coach. He had done nothing more than take advantage of her willingness. In all that long and glorious night he had never whispered to her of love. She thought of the long list of his amours, ending with Lady Bradwell, and her doubts increased.

The afternoon dragged by for Diana, torn as she was by her doubts, and Alexander did not return. Finally, in late afternoon, she ordered the grays harnessed for a ride in the park. She had buttoned her pelisse and was standing just inside the door putting on her kid gloves under the watchful eye of a footman when Alexander suddenly arrived.

His face was tired and drawn, and so was the smile he gave her. "Where are you going?"

"For a ride in the park." She hoped she had managed to keep her disappointment at his perfunctory greeting from her face. It had confirmed her worst fears.

"Don't let me keep you." He turned and headed upstairs.

As she left the house, she very nearly collided with a breathless youth who demanded to know whether she was the duchess of Stratford.

Much taken aback, she admitted she was.

The youth whipped an envelope from his gray wool jacket, much spotted and worn. "I'm to place this in your hands and none other's," he announced as he handed her the envelope with a flourish. "And I'm to wait for your answer."

Annoyed by his brashness, she started to tell him there would be no answer; then her eye saw the squarish handwriting, and with a sinking heart she tore open the letter. It was, as she feared, from Antoine, and it was brief. He was in London, and she was to meet him that afternoon in the park so that they might plan their elopement. It concluded: "I told you I would rescue you from the duke. You see how wise we were to wait until you had married, for now we shall be able to claim your fortune."

Two red spots of fury burned on Diana's cheeks as she read the message. She crumpled up the paper and stuffed it into her reticule. She marched back into the house and to a writing table in one of the small sitting rooms. There, seizing paper and pen, she scribbled hastily, "I never want to see or hear from you again, Antoine. I despise you." Sealing her message, she returned to the hall and handed it to the youth with a pound note. "Here is your answer. See that you deliver it."

After the door closed behind the youth, she hesitated for a moment. She dared not go riding in the park now, or Antoine would think she had come to meet him, after all. Yet if she did not go out after announcing her intentions to Alexander, she would arouse his suspicions, and she most fervently did not want him to ever again hear of Antoine. He had already caused enough trouble between her and her husband.

In the end, instead of going to the park, she directed the grays toward Bond Street, where she passed an hour in aimless shopping.

She bought nothing. Indeed, she hardly saw the tempting wares before her, so lost was she in her fear that Alexander would learn Antoine was in London and had contacted her. She was still much distressed when she returned to Stratford House. How would she get through the evening without betraying her agitation to Alexander? She was thankful that they were to go to the theater that night. She prayed that she would be able to conceal her roiling emotions in its darkness.

In her apartment, she pulled Antoine's crumpled note from her reticule.

"Diana."

Alexander's voice from the door behind her made her jump in surprise. She heard him coming across the floor toward her. Hastily, she opened the drawer of her writing table and tossed the note into it before he could see it.

He touched her shoulder. "I want to skip the theater tonight and go to Arthur Dowman's instead. I understand he is having a particularly brilliant group. Would you mind?''

Normally, she would have been delighted at the chance to go to Dowman's. Their evenings spent there were her particular favorites. But in her present agitation, she could not face such a gathering with its demands on her. The thought of having to be bright and witty while in her current state of fear and confusion was more than she could contemplate. She turned to face her husband. ''I would mind very much indeed.''

He was obviously startled by the sharpness of her tone. ''Please, Diana, I would much prefer not to go to the theater.''

''And I much prefer to,'' she cried, trying to keep the panic from her voice. ''I have been so looking forward to seeing Mrs. Siddons perform tonight. It is said to be her best role in years. Please, Alexander, you promised.''

''If you absolutely insist,'' he said reluctantly, ''we will go.''

''I do absolutely insist,'' she said firmly.

''Very well.'' His face was creased with displeasure as he turned and vanished into his own room.

As Diana sat at her dressing table putting the final touches to her toilette for the theater, Alexander reappeared. To her astonishment, he draped around her neck the most spectacular diamond necklace she had ever seen.

''The Stratford diamonds,'' he told her curtly, without preamble. ''Wear them tonight.''

Puzzled by his abruptness, she protested that the necklace was too showy for the theater.

He replied in a voice that brooked no opposition, ''If you insist that we go to the theater, I insist that you wear it. Your choice, my duchess.''

He had not been so curt toward her since their marriage. Stung by his manner, she retorted, ''I am amazed that you still have such a piece as this in your possession. I would have supposed that you long ago would have given it to one or another of your inamoratas.''

Alexander's face hardened. ''The diamonds are entailed. They are part of the Stratford estate.'' He turned on his heel and stalked out.

Tears welled up in her eyes. It was as if the previous night—all of the passion and the pleasure that they had shared—had never happened. Now that she had become another one of his conquests, he had immediately lost interest in her. What other explanation could there be for the sudden change in him? Unless—she shuddered—he had somehow heard that Antoine was in London. She told herself that was impossible. But she was not entirely convinced.

The ride to the theater was tense and silent. Alexander was still in evil humor, and his duchess was assailed by a new terror. What if Antoine should be at the theater?

As they entered, she found herself searching the crowd anxiously. To her relief she saw no one resembling Antoine, or at least Antoine as she remembered him. Nevertheless, she was relieved when she reached their box and grateful for the friends who stopped by the box to greet her and her husband. Her diamond necklace drew many envious glances and compliments.

Just as the curtain was about to rise on the first act, a woman of such exquisite beauty that every head turned toward her entered a box across from Stratford's. Never had Diana seen such a ravishing creature. Her remarkable face was surrounded by clouds of rich brown-black hair, her large green eyes were framed by dark lashes, and her mouth was sensuous and inviting. She was wearing a rich cloak of green velvet trimmed with sable.

Diana turned to quip to Alexander that now she knew what Helen of Troy's face, which had launched a thousand ships, must have looked like. But something in Alexander's face, the way his mouth was drawn in tight lines, made her pause, as did the fact that every man in the theater was staring appreciatively at the newcomer except Alexander.

Slowly, the woman loosened her cloak, and as it slipped from her shoulders, Diana saw the necklace of huge, perfectly matched emeralds that glittered at her beautiful throat and very nearly matched her gleaming green eyes. Diana's stomach churned, and she felt faint. Although she had heard that Lady Bradwell was a beauty, she had never expected such a breathtaking creature as now sat in the box across from her.

Diana knew that once she herself had eschewed the dreadful makeup that she had used to dull her complexion and her hair, which she now wore in a more flattering style, she was by any standards very pretty. This realization was not vanity on her part but honesty. But Lady Bradwell was such an exquisitely beautiful creature that Diana felt suddenly dowdy and plain.

A stricken Diana watched as her husband glanced casually at Lady Bradwell without appearing to betray the slightest interest, then turned to his wife and began talking about the night's program. Diana could only marvel at her husband's cool poise. He was the only man in the theater whose eyes were not fixed on Lady Bradwell, who herself, now that she was settled in her box, had eyes only for Alexander. She gave Diana the superior glance of a woman who has measured her rival and found her wanting. Then Lady Bradwell's gaze lowered, and she gave a start at the sight of the spectacular diamond necklace that Diana wore, grander even than the emeralds. Only in the necklace did Diana's appearance eclipse her husband's mistress.

As the curtain went up, Diana's heart weighed like a heavy boulder in her chest as she understood why Alexander had insisted she wear the diamonds. He had known Lady Bradwell would be at the theater, and it would never do to have the jewels he had given to his mistress outshine those worn by the wife at his side. Yet how could he have known that Lady Bradwell would be there unless she had told him? So now Diana knew where Alexander had been all day. He must have gone directly from his wife's bed to his mistress. Diana was thankful for the concealment the darkened theater offered her. No one could see the tears that she could not keep from her eyes. She could never hope to compete in Alexander's eyes with such a beauty as Lady Bradwell. Diana's cheeks burned with humiliation as she thought of the intensity with which she had enjoyed and returned her husband's lovemaking the night before. What a fool she had been to think that he cared about her as anything more than a convenience to fill his pockets and his nursery.

The intermission was agony for Diana. Most of the audience was watching the two boxes containing Lady Bradwell and the Stratfords with unflagging interest, their eyes traveling from one to the other in open curiosity. Alexander ignored it all, chatting resolutely to Diana about the performances, the stage sets, and various mutual acquaintances. She marveled at his seemingly careless indifference to all the eyes upon them. But she could not act so cooly.

"Please," she begged finally, "take me home. I cannot bear it here."

"No," he said sharply, under his breath. "You were the one who insisted upon coming. Now you shall have to see it out."

"You knew that she would be here tonight, didn't you?"

"Yes," he said curtly.

Diana wondered numbly how a single word like that could break her heart, but that is what it had done, for it had confirmed to her that her suspicions of where Alexander had spent the day were correct. The previous night had meant so little to him that he had gone directly from Diana's bed to his mistress. It took all her willpower to keep her voice steady.

"That's why you insisted I wear the diamonds tonight, isn't it?"

"Yes," he said between his teeth, and turned to greet a visitor who had stopped at the back of the box.

As they rode home after the theater, Alexander doggedly persevered in discussing the night's production, although he could elicit nothing more than an occasional monosyllable from his wife.

Finally, he demanded in exasperation, "What is the matter with you? Can't you say anything?"

Diana stiffened, haunted by the vision of Lady Bradwell, so confident of her loveliness, sitting triumphantly in her box and glorying in the admiration of the audience. Undoubtedly, in their eyes and in her husband's, just as in Diana's own eyes, she was a poor second to his mistress.

"Lady Bradwell's emerald necklace is very beautiful," Diana answered sullenly.

Alexander flushed. "I am sick of hearing about those damned emeralds. Don't ever mention them to me again." He sank back angrily against the green velvet cushions of the carriage.

"You might have warned me she would be there," Diana said.

"Would you have stayed away? I don't think so."

Alexander was right, Diana realized. Curious to see her rival, whom she had not imagined to be quite so exquisite, she would have still insisted upon going. Nor would it have occurred to Diana, as it had obviously occurred to her husband, that they would attract more attention than the actors on stage.

"She is very beautiful." Diana said in a small voice.

"Yes, she is," Alexander agreed curtly, and lapsed into silence.

Diana swallowed hard, unable to speak for the huge lump

in her throat. They completed the ride without another word spoken between them.

When they reached home, the footman who opened the door for them handed Diana on a little silver plate an envelope addressed to her. With sinking heart she recognized Antoine's squarish, back-slanting handwriting. She took it and started hastily up the stairs.

"Aren't you going to open it?" Alexander asked behind her.

She continued up the stairs. "I am certain whatever it is, it is of no importance." She tried to sound airy but failed miserably. She was relieved when they reached the ducal apartments that Alexander did not follow her into her chamber but went into his own.

Once she was alone, she hastily tore open Antoine's message and read, "I shall see you in the morning. Love, Antoine."

Diana was furious at his persistence. She would not see him. She would instruct the butler the next day that Antoine was to be turned away if he came to the door. Crumpling his message, she tossed it into the drawer with his other note. She was uneasy about throwing them away. What if a curious servant might notice them and read their contents?

Diana lay in her bed, furious at her husband but longing for the warmth of his body beside her. She cringed in embarrassment as she recalled how she had flung herself at him the night before and he had condescended to accept her.

Sleep would not come to her, and sometime later, her emotions still churning, she heard a noise. Turning her head on her thick down pillows, she saw Alexander in a robe standing in the connecting doorway between their chambers.

"What do you want?" she asked, a tiny quiver in her voice.

"You know what I want." His tone was mocking. "It is

what every husband wants, and it is his wife's duty to provide.''

His answer infuriated her, and she snapped, ''That and my money, too, my lord duke. How greedy you are.''

He sighed. ''I thought you would realize I was teasing you, Diana. What nasty humor you are in tonight.'' He shed his robe and slipped into the bed beside her. She tried to push him away, but he enveloped her in an embrace, observing, ''You were not so uneager last night.''

She thought of Lady Bradwell. ''Things have changed since last night.''

His voice against her ear was suddenly harsh. ''What do you mean?''

Diana realized with despair that he would never understand how she felt. He treated her for all the world to see as his cherished and cosseted duchess. Nor could she have any complaint about his generosity to her. For a man of his rank, it was quite the accepted thing to keep a mistress or two on the side. He would never understand how repugnant it was to her to share his lovemaking with any woman.

''Nothing,'' she said bitterly, and tried again to pull away from him.

But he was not to be rebuffed. The gentle patience of the night before was gone. Instead, he was urgent, demanding, possessive. He ignored and finally overwhelmed her feeble opposition. She found herself responding against her will, clinging to him as she had the previous morning, moaning with pleasure.

When their passion was spent, he lay back on the pillow and whispered, ''I think things have not changed so much since last night.'' Then he was fast asleep.

CHAPTER 22

When Diana arose the next morning, Alexander was gone on some unspecified business, which, in her distressed state, she was certain was Lady Bradwell.

Diana was sitting in a blue velvet dressing gown in her bedchamber, sipping her morning chocolate, her long blond hair still hanging loosely about her, when her maid appeared. Holding out a calling card, the young woman announced that a gentleman wished to see Her Grace. Diana took the card. She gasped as she saw Antoine's name printed on it in crisp black letters. Despite his message the night before, she had not expected him to appear so early.

"Tell him I am not at home," she said.

The little maid looked frightened. "He most particularly bade me to tell Your Grace that he knew you were home and that he would not leave until he had seen you. He is not, I think, a nice man."

What if Alexander should return and find Antoine there? Diana shuddered at what her husband's reaction would be to that. Antoine's name had not passed between them since the day of their marriage, and Diana's liveliest desire was that her husband never again be reminded of anything connected with her sorry attempt to elope.

Weak with anxiety, Diana said, "Tell the gentleman I wish never to see him again."

"I am already here," a heavily accented voice said.

Diana looked up in shock to see Antoine standing at the door that led from her sitting room.

The maid pushed her hands against her face in horror at the outrageous intrusion.

Diana, looking as though she had seen an apparition, rose to her feet so hastily that she upset her cup of chocolate, but in her shock she did not even notice the brown liquid spreading over the table and dripping down onto the Aubusson carpet. "How dare you come in here, Antoine? Leave at once or I shall have you thrown out." She moved toward him, determined to prevent him from intruding any farther into her bedchamber.

"*Non.* You hear me first, eh. I risk too much to get this far." Although Antoine wrote perfectly correct, if formal and somewhat stilted, English, he spoke it with less skill and more accent. He nodded at the maid. "Get rid of the creature."

Diana noticed for the first time the dripping chocolate. "Anna," she told the frightened maid, "clean up that mess, please." To Antoine, Diana said firmly, "While she is doing that, we will talk in the sitting room."

They retreated into her private sitting room, where he turned upon her with blazing eyes. The years had not been kind to Antoine. The face that Diana had once thought so handsome had thickened, and a faint scar across his cheek gave him a rather sinister look. The smile that years before had enchanted her had settled into a habitual sneer. He had about him the tiny, almost imperceptible signs of a man who had come upon hard times. Although he obviously had taken great pains with his appearance, his brown cloth coat with the velvet collar was shiny with the telltale signs of long wear and much brushing. His leather boots with the wide brown cuffs, although carefully polished, also were well worn and slightly run-down at the heels. He demanded roughly, "Why did you not meet me in the park yesterday, eh?"

She shut the door to the bedchamber firmly behind her so that the maid could not overhear their conversation. "I did not want ever to set eyes on you again, Antoine. I told you so in the note that I wrote you."

"Why? You are willing enough to run off with me before, *n'est-ce pas?*"

"What a low opinion you must hold of me. Did you seriously think I would marry a man merely to secure my fortune, then abandon him and my marriage vows to run off with a scapegrace like you who wants nothing but my money?"

Antoine had not sufficient conscience to be abashed by her indictment of him. Nor did he deny it. Instead, he lashed out in a rush of anger. "Do you know what I risk coming here, not just to England but all the way to London, to see you? You lead me on, you double-dealing witch. Now you try to shut the door in my face."

"It was you who failed me. It was you who did not come when I so desperately counted upon your help. But you did not care about that. All that mattered to you was my fortune."

Antoine shrugged with a bit of that old nonchalance that Diana had once found so charming. "*Eh bien*, why be poor when we can be rich?" His face hardened, making the scar on his cheek more apparent. "Napoleon confiscated what little I have. You think it is romantic to be poor, eh? But it is wretched."

She said nothing, only glared at him with stony hatred.

Seeing her hostility, he tried to placate her. "It is only you I think of, *ma chérie*. I cannot bear for you to want for anything. Let us stop this foolish arguing and plan our escape. There is no time to lose, for we rendezvous before dawn with the smuggler's ship that carries us to safety."

Diana glared at him with mingled disgust and disbelief. "You are an even greater fool than I thought to believe that I would run away from my husband and place myself under your dubious protection now that I know what an evil, unscrupulous man you are."

His face whitened in rage, and the scar stood out, a livid streak, against his skin. "By God, you come with me." He grabbed her roughly and pulled her to him. "I do not risk a hanging to come away empty-handed." He bent his head, and his mouth, stinking of cheap tobacco, attacked hers with a bruising kiss that filled her with as much revulsion as Alexander's had filled her with pleasure.

She struggled to escape him, but he had her arms pinned to her sides. She tried to wrench her lips away from his awful mouth, but he put his hand behind her head and held it as though it were in a vise, forcing her to accept his disgusting kiss.

She heard the door open. She tried to cry for help from whoever was there, but Antoine's mouth over hers swallowed any sound from her lips.

"What the devil!" she heard a man exclaim angrily.

Antoine released his grip on Diana's head and turned his own to see who was at the door. To Diana's horror, standing in the doorway beside the little maid Anna was her brother-in-law, Lord Charles Hadleigh. Charlie's usually cheerful countenance was glazed with shock.

Diana shoved Antoine away from her. "Get out of here, you—" She broke off, unable to think of any term sufficiently vile to bestow upon Antoine.

Antoine gave her an exaggerated bow. Then, with a smirk in the direction of the doorway, he said for the benefit of the audience there, "My love, you must train your servants they are not to disturb us." He sauntered to the door.

Passing Charlie, Antoine bowed to him. "If you will permit me, *mon bon monsieur,* your timing is atrocious. You have spoiled a most pleasurable interlude." He disappeared through the door, leaving three pairs of astounded eyes staring after him.

Diana was bereft of speech by Antoine's audacious behavior and brazen lies.

Her brother-in-law turned and gazed angrily upon her. His furious look took in her disheveled hair hanging long and loose about her shoulders and the velvet dressing gown she was wearing. She was acutely aware of how compromising the situation must appear to him.

Diana, who had never fainted in her life, suddenly felt very faint indeed. So faint that it was a moment before she could gather the strength to rise from the sofa. "Oh, that evil, lying wretch," she moaned.

"Those did not appear to be your sentiments a moment ago." The contempt in Charlie's usually placid voice sent her heart plummeting to her ankles.

"He forced himself upon me, Charlie," she cried.

"That Frenchman—at least I gather from his accent that is what he is—did not take his leave like a man who had just committed assault."

"He is a consummate actor," Diana said bitterly, remembering how talented he had been in the plays at Tante Germaine's.

"One or the other of you is." Charlie's face, usually so cheerful, was grim. "For my brother's sake, I would like to believe you. I cannot bear for Alex to be so betrayed by the first woman he ever loved."

"Loved!" Diana cried in disbelief, so shocked by his words that she forgot Antoine. "Ah, yes, he loves me so much that he cannot stay away from Lady Bradwell."

It was Charlie's turn to be surprised. "Lady Bradwell bores him," he said flatly.

Hope flared within Diana's breast, then died. "Bores him so much he gave her an emerald necklace worth a king's ransom after he was betrothed to me."

"My brother's greatest fault and one of his most engaging characteristics is his generosity. He can never turn down a supplication, and he loves giving presents." Charlie pulled a tiny enameled snuffbox from his pocket. "Besides, I should be delighted about that necklace if I were you."

Diana stared at him as if he had taken leave of his senses. "Delighted!"

Charlie nodded. "It was Alex's farewell gift to her. He is

famous for giving his convenients some fabulous bauble when he is finished with them. It is rather his trademark.''

Diana desperately wanted to believe Charlie, but when she thought of her husband's unexplained absences, she was unpersuaded. ''He is still seeing Lady Bradwell,'' she insisted stubbornly.

''I have given up gambling,'' Charlie said, ''but I would wager you any sum you care to name that Alex has not visited Angela since your marriage.''

''You are wrong. He visited her only yesterday.''

Charlie snapped open the snuffbox. ''What would make you think that?

''Alexander knew that she would be at the theater last night.''

''Of course he knew, because I told him she would be there. She has been trying desperately to set up some sort of confrontation between you and her ever since your marriage. She hoped to accomplish it at the theater last night. I heard about it and warned Alex. Surely you did not go there. Alex said he would not.''

''I insisted we go,'' she replied in a tiny voice.

''How hateful that must have been for Alex.''

''For Alex?'' she exclaimed.

''He has tried so hard to smother all the dreadful gossip that circulated about your marriage and to shield you from any unpleasantness. To go to the theater last night was to court it.'' Charlie took a pinch of snuff and inhaled it. ''Furthermore, for all Alex's apparent indifference, he despises being stared at and gossiped about, and I am certain you must have been the center of attention.''

''He acted so unconcerned,'' she said, at last beginning to understand why her husband had been in such bad humor the previous night and what his nonchalance in the theater must have cost him. She marveled at how coolly he had brought it off. He would not be so cool, however, if Charlie were to tell him about the wretched scene he had just witnessed. Her only hope of making her brother-in-law understand and keep his silence was to tell him all that had happened.

"Charlie," she began, but was stopped by the door opening. She suppressed a groan as she saw Alexander come in.

He greeted his brother warmly. "Charlie, what a pleasant surprise. Diana, the countess of Custis has come to call on you and is waiting downstairs." Alexander smiled affectionately at her. "And you're not even dressed yet. Hurry along while I entertain Charlie."

She stood as though turned to stone. She wanted a moment alone with Charlie to assure him how much she loved his brother and to beg him to say nothing of what he had seen until she could at least tell him the whole story.

"Hurry, Diana," Alexander said impatiently. "You are keeping the countess waiting."

Diana had to content herself with a pleading look at Charlie as she left them. While she dressed and throughout her seemingly interminable visit with the countess, she prayed that Charlie would say nothing to his brother about Antoine.

But when she returned to her apartments after the countess's departure, she found Alexander waiting for her alone in her sitting room. He was seated at her writing desk, the two crumpled notes from Antoine spread out before him on its inlaid surface. His face was harsh with fury. "What a bold one you are, having an assignation with your lover in your own apartment in your husband's house."

She faltered before his rage. "It was not an assignation. It was not at all what you think."

The right eyebrow arched to soaring heights of disbelief. "What an interesting notion you have of how a lady should entertain gentlemen callers." His voice dripped with sarcasm. "You greet them, your hair streaming about your shoulders, in your dressing gown in your bedchamber and shower them with kisses."

"I swear it was not at all like that." Tears welled up in her eyes. "He pushed his way in."

"But despite this want of conduct, you did not see fit to summon a servant to eject him? I presume your caller was Antoine."

She nodded miserably.

Alexander picked up one of Antoine's notes and waved it at her. "And I suppose you did not meet Antoine in the park yesterday afternoon, either."

"No, I did not," she cried. How could she ever make him believe the truth?

"Let me remind you that when you left the house yesterday afternoon, you yourself told me you were going for a ride in the park." He threw the note down on the writing table and jumped up, bumping his leg painfully. But he hardly seemed to notice.

"I changed my mind when I got Antoine's note. It was delivered to me as I left the house. I did not want to see him, nor did I see him. I went shopping in Pall Mall instead of going to the park."

Alexander had begun pacing up and down with short, angry steps. "What did you buy?"

"Nothing," she confessed.

He stopped his pacing and confronted her with furious gray eyes. "You expect me to believe such a preposterous story as that?"

"It is the truth," she cried as he began pacing again. But she knew that in his place she would not have believed her tale, either. Through her tears, she stared at the wrinkled notes on the writing table and stammered, "I would think you would be above going through my desk, reading my discarded notes."

Alexander whirled on her in fury. "I am not above it when I discover I am being cuckolded. Oh, God, and to think how I loved you."

He stalked from the room, down the stairs, and out of the house.

Diana sank down on the sofa, that last terrible look he gave her and his final words seared into her soul.

CHAPTER 23

For a long time after Alexander had stormed out of the house, Diana sat on the fatal sofa in her sitting room, her mind in a muddle. Alex loved her. He had said it. Charlie had said it. It was the core around which all her thoughts spun. Could it really be true? If he loved her, why had he waited so long to demonstrate that love in their marriage bed? And even if it had been true that he had loved her, was it still the case, or had Antoine destroyed Alexander's regard for her? Only one thing was certain: she had never wanted anything so much in her life as she wanted her husband.

Somehow she would have to force him to believe the truth of what she told him. But she was well aware how impossible it was to force the duke of Stratford to do anything. Her chin tilted upright at a determined angle. Somehow she would convince him of her innocence and of her great love for him.

As the hours passed and Alexander did not return, Diana grew increasingly nervous. She had a fitting in the late afternoon for the gown that she was to wear to her father's wedding to Isabel, now only a week away.

Diana wandered about her apartments, too agitated to do

anything but agonize over what would happen when Alexander returned. Finally, she went through the connecting door between their rooms and into his bedchamber. To her surprise, she saw that the door to the locked room was standing open. As she came in, the duke's valet emerged from it.

Barlow was much taken aback to see her and hastily shut the door.

"Why is that door kept locked?"

The valet shrugged his shoulders impassively. "His Grace's orders."

"But why?"

"He wishes no one to know its purpose."

"Is it so nefarious as that, that it must be kept a secret and locked away?" she cried, genuinely shocked.

Barlow squirmed in great discomfort. "It is nothing bad," he hastened to assure her.

"Then you can tell me what it is. After all, I am His Grace's wife."

Her argument seemed to convince the valet. He said slowly, "It is His Grace's studio for his sculpture."

"Sculpture?" Diana would more readily have believed bodies were buried in the room. "Surely you jest. His Grace is no sculptor."

Barlow's loyalty to his master outweighed his reticence. "He is a fine sculptor. Not that he does much of it. The only time he used that room in recent months was when he made that present for you."

"The bust of Portia?" Diana gasped.

"Made both them busts in the drawing room, he did. Quite a time he had with the one for you. His Grace has always been a perfectionist, but I've never seen him so fussy about anything as he was that piece. Worked on it day and night, he did. Afraid he would not finish it by the time you came up to London."

Diana could get no words past the great lump in her

throat. She remembered how anxious Alexander had been that she should like the bust of Portia. Now that she knew he had sculpted it especially to please her, it claimed an even deeper hold on her heart—and so did its creator.

No wonder Alexander had been so astonished that day at Greycote when he had discovered the Hamlet. A smile twitched at her lips as she recalled his discomfort as she sought to draw praise of the unknown sculptor from him. Modesty was not a trait that she had suspected Alexander possessed.

By now her view of her husband had undergone such a radical change that she wanted nothing so much as the opportunity to hold him again in her arms.

But when the time came for Diana to leave for her fitting, Alexander still had not returned.

She had dressed with special care in a blue silk gown that she knew was a particular favorite of her husband's. Small floral sprigs of white-and-green Chinese embroidery decorated the bodice and the voluminous skirt. Over it, she donned a short, fitted spencer jacket of blue velvet that ended at her waist. Her hat was a wide-brimmed bonnet trimmed in a blue velvet ribbon that matched the spencer. She pulled on kid gloves and went down the steps of Stratford House to her waiting carriage.

To her surprise, a new coachman had replaced Tebbets on the box.

"Where is Tebbets?" she asked in concern.

"He be ailing, and I be taking his place for the day," replied the new man, a big coarse fellow with stringy black hair and tobacco-stained teeth.

He was not at all the sort of man she would have expected her husband to have in his employ, but obviously he had been drafted from the stables for the day.

"What is wrong with Tebbets?" Diana asked.

"It be his chest, an inflammation. He were told he were

on no account to work in this weather or 'twill be the death of him.''

Diana settled into the velvet-cushioned carriage, glad for the comfort of the fur rug, which she wrapped about her. The day had turned gray and sullen. She rather regretted not having worn her sable-trimmed pelisse, which would have been so much warmer than the short spencer.

She pulled the velvet curtains of the carriage shut to close out the depressing day and sank back into the cushions and her own unhappy thoughts.

She paid no heed to the carriage's route until a rank odor of decaying garbage assailed her nostrils. Parting the curtains, she was astonished to discover that she was in an alley littered with foul, rotting refuse behind a row of grime-encrusted brick buildings. Iron bars instead of glass protected their small windows. She was in a most wretched part of London, although she had no idea which one.

The coach suddenly jerked to a stop with such violence that she was pitched forward against the seat across from her. Before she could recover her seat, the coach door banged open, and Antoine jumped in.

He grabbed for her. Realizing her danger, she pulled up her knees, aimed her feet at his chest, and gave as mighty a shove as she could manage. Caught off-balance, he fell back out of the coach and would have landed hard on the ground on his backside had not the coachman, who had climbed down from the box, caught him and helped him regain his feet.

Diana threw open the door on the other side of the carriage and leaped out. Looking hastily about her, she saw that the alley was sealed at one end by a red brick building and that the only way out lay behind her. Another coach, this one a nondescript vehicle battered from long, hard usage, had been pulled across the alley's exit and waited with its door open.

She began to run as fast as her long, voluminous skirts would permit her toward the one possible avenue of escape. The slimy muck that covered the cobblestones made them very slippery, adding to her difficulties. She could hear Antoine's curses and two pairs of running feet, growing ever closer, behind her.

Ten paces from the alley's exit, she slipped on a piece of garbage that had been tossed there and fell headlong onto the filth of the cobblestones. As she fell, she saw two ragged children and a scrawny, bleak-faced woman goggling at her. "Help!" she screamed at them as she struggled to her knees.

But Antoine was immediately upon her, knocking her back down on the slimy cobblestones with such force that her wide-brimmed bonnet tumbled off. He straddled her, and his hand closed over her mouth, silencing her. She twisted beneath him and tried to claw at his face, but her nails were sheathed by her kid gloves. She tried to pummel him with her fists, but he seemed impervious to her blows.

Finally, she succeeded in sinking her teeth deep into his hand over her mouth. He yelped in pain and withdrew it. She screamed again. His hands closed around her throat, choking both breath and voice from her. He was going to kill her, she thought as she struggled in vain to wrest his hands from her neck.

As she was slipping into unconsciousness, she heard the coachman snarl at the woman and children, "Get out of here and forget what you saw or I'll knock your bloody heads in."

CHAPTER 24

Slowly, Diana regained consciousness, her head throbbing. Her mind was spinning in confusion, and she could not immediately comprehend what was happening to her. It took her a bit to realize that the jostling she felt was more than the swimming in her head and that she was in a coach racing over rough roads. Her eyes still seemed so heavy that she could not immediately force the lids open. She had no idea how long she had been unconscious. Her throat hurt so that it was painful even to breathe.

When finally she opened her eyes, the world twirled around her like a spinning top. Blinking hard, she tried to focus her eyes. Succeeding finally, she saw that the carriage lamp was lit, indicating that night had fallen. In the faint light cast by the lamp she saw Antoine on the seat across from her. She closed her eyes again quickly to blot out his hated countenance.

She was lying across a seat. The material beneath her head was not the softness of the velvet that lined Alexander's carriage but rather a worn, cracked leather. She remembered the coach that had been drawn across the mouth of the alley and presumed that was the vehicle in which they were now riding. The plan must have been to stop in the alley and transfer her from her husband's distinctive, highly polished carriage with the ducal crest upon the door to a less conspicuous vehicle.

She tried to move and discovered that her hands had been tied in front of her and that her legs, too, had been hobbled.

Diana had no doubt what Antoine's plans were for her. Even now they must be racing toward the coast where he must rendezvous with the smugglers' ship before dawn the following day. He would force her aboard with him. The captain would have no scruples about an unwilling passenger so long as he was compensated.

While Diana could guess what Antoine was doing, she could not understand why he was doing it. What did he hope to gain by dragging her with him?

When would she first be missed? It could be hours, and at the breakneck speed the coach was traveling, she could be beyond saving by the time it was even discovered that she was gone. And would her husband care?

For of greater concern to her even than what might lay ahead of her with Antoine was what Alexander might think. He had left the house in a rage that morning, thinking her already consorting with Antoine. Would her sudden disappearance confirm his darkest doubts of her?

She opened her eyes a second time and was rewarded with a smirk from Antoine. "So, *ma chérie*, you decide to awake, eh. What a long sleep you take."

"You will never succeed in this, Antoine." Diana was surprised at how painful it was to force words through her bruised throat. Nevertheless, she managed to inject a conviction into her voice that she was far from feeling in her heart. "My husband will come after us, and he will kill you."

In the coach's pale lamplight, Antoine's eyes gleamed with malicious triumph. "I think he not come after us, not after he reads the letter you write him, *ma chérie*."

"Letter?" she demanded in alarm. "What letter? You will never force me to write him."

"But you already write him the letter, *ma chérie*, and a work of art, it is. Five pounds it costs me. I hire a forger clever enough to imitate your handwriting from the letter you send me from Greycote." Antoine pulled from his pocket a cheap metal watch and consulted it. "The letter, it is delivered now." He snapped the case shut and put the watch back in his pocket.

A wave of horror swept over Diana. "What," she whispered, "did the letter say?"

"The letter assures your husband that you always adore me and hate him. You go along with your marriage to him only to allay suspicion. All the protestations you make to him of your affection are a lie to delude him and to help us escape. The letter describes in detail his defects that you write me of—the arrogance, the conceit, the contempt of women. It is a masterful indictment of him, masterful."

"No, no," she moaned in despair, knowing that her marriage to Alexander had ended the moment he had opened that letter. She wanted to die. Never had Alexander been so dear to her, nor had she loved him so much, as in that moment, when she knew that she had lost him forever.

With great difficulty because of her bound hands, she tried to struggle to a sitting position.

"But let me help you, *ma chérie,* eh." Antoine seized her arms and raised her so that she was seated upon the leather cushion.

Diana shrank from his disgusting touch. Miserably, she wondered what Alexander would do. Divorce her quietly, no doubt.

She looked down at her lap and realized to her horror that most of the blue silk skirt of her gown had been torn away and that she was in her petticoats. "What has happened to my gown?" she gasped.

Antoine shrugged. "It was covered with muck. I tore it away so that the filth would not soil the coach."

Her eyes, filled with hatred, blazed at Antoine. "What can you possibly hope to gain by abducting me?"

"Your fortune, of course. You write me that you inherit it once you marry."

She began to laugh hysterically. "You fool, you stupid fool. The money did not come to me; it came to my husband. The terms of my grandfather's will were very clear that the money was to be placed fully in my husband's control. You will never see any of it.''

He started forward, grabbed her, shook her fiercely. *"Mon Dieu,"* he gasped. "You lie, surely you lie.''

"I do not lie," she assured him vehemently. Her only vengeance on Antoine for ruining her marriage, her reputation, and her life would be that he would never get his greedy hands on the fortune for which he was willing to risk so much. "My money remains with my husband.''

"Then he shall pay royally to get you back.''

She laughed bitterly at the thought of what reaction such a demand would elicit from Alexander after he had read the forged letter. "You are an even greater fool than I thought, Antoine. He will be delighted that you have rid him of me and assured him my fortune in the bargain. He would not pay you a ha'pence for my return.''

Antoine's face turned ashen, making his scar a red slash in the lamplight. A sudden desperate plan formed in Diana's mind. If only she could convince Antoine to release her since she would bring him no monetary gain.

"Let me go, Antoine. You cannot hope to get anything from my husband for my return, and I only hamper your escape. You have a long way to go, and I doubt the smugglers will wait for you. If you abandon me and the coach and take the horses, how much better your chance will be of getting away.''

He thought over her argument, his greedy eyes searching her face for any sign of deception. Finally, he said stubbornly, *"Non.* I come for you, and I leave with you.''

"But of what possible value can I be to you? I am only a hindrance.''

"True, but perhaps the husband is not so unwilling to bargain. And if he is . . .'' Antoine shrugged, and his hands darted out, burying themselves in her hair, which had half tumbled down from its pins. She tried to jerk her head free from him, but he grabbed a large handful of hair and pulled it back until she moaned with pain. With his free hand, he removed what pins remained so that her hair cascaded down in a golden cloud down about her. He eyed her appreciatively in the dim lamplight of the coach. "I find someone who is willing to pay a good price for such a fine piece as you."

The realization of what he meant sickened her, but she was determined that she would not be cowed. "I despise you, and I shall never stop fighting you, Antoine, never. I promise you that."

"You frighten me, madame," he mocked.

The wheels of the coach struck a deep hole, bouncing its occupants about hard on the seat. How uncomfortable the smelly coach was after Alexander's well-sprung carriage, now abandoned in a wretched London alley. And where was Tebbets? Had he been left lying in some alley, too, after he was waylaid?

When Diana asked about Tebbets, Antoine only shrugged and said, "He is of no matter."

The answer frightened Diana. "Have you killed him?"

Antoine shrugged again. "Perhaps."

She glared at him with loathing. How right her mother had been about Antoine's character. Why, oh, why, had Diana not believed her instead of Antoine's lies?

The coach suddenly lurched to a stop. The door opened to disclose in the pale lamplight a youth in worn cotton pantaloons held up by a rope at the waist. Antoine got out of the coach and talked to the boy in low tones. Diana could catch only snatches of the conversation but gathered that he would act as some kind of guide.

Antoine got back into the coach, and the boy climbed up on the box beside the coarse coachman. The coach lurched forward again.

The air was heavy now with the salt tang and fish odor of

the sea. The road was rougher, deeply rutted, and the coach was forced to slow its pace. Finally, it stopped altogether. Antoine forced Diana out of the coach with him. The night was so dark, without moon or stars, that she could not see the youth scamper down from the box. She could only hear him.

She could hear, too, the crash of the sea below them and surmised that they were standing on a palisade above the ocean.

The youth started down a barely discernible path, and Antoine pushed Diana after him. She heard the coach start up again and drive off in the darkness. They would have no more need of it or its coarse driver. The ocean would be their road now.

As they followed the youth, a wiry figure with slightly bowed legs, loose rocks slid away beneath their feet.

With her bound hands and her long skirts, Diana had great difficulty making her way on the steep, treacherous path that led down a gap between two headlands. Several times she stumbled, and Antoine caught her roughly. Once he was not quick enough, and she went sprawling in the dirt, the cruel little stones scraping her painfully. Cursing her violently in French, Antoine seized her and jerked her roughly to her feet. "You try to delay us," he accused her bitterly.

"I cannot help it with my hands tied and my long skirts," She would not let him intimidate her. "Untie my hands, then."

Instead, he grabbed the back of her pelisse and pushed her in front of him as they half walked, half slid down the treacherous path. The spines of sea buckthorn caught at her clothes and scratched her face.

Now Antoine was cursing the boy, whose name it appeared was Tom. Diana gathered he served as a smugglers' lookout and knew every inch of that part of the coast as a pastor knows his Bible.

"Surely there is an easier way down than this," Antoine complained. "The stairs—are there none?"

"There are, just beyond that headland." The youth nodded his head to his left. "But there's most always a guard, too. What with all the smugglers that be plying this coast, they watch the easy places closest."

Finally, they reached the bottom of the path and stepped into soft sand. The clouds drifted momentarily away from the moon, and in the meager light Diana saw that they were on a narrow crescent of beach, trapped between the cliffs and the sea. Not more than three feet of sand lay between the base of the rocks and the strandline marked by deposits of rotting seaweed.

Diana shivered, knowing that somewhere out there lay a ship that would take her away from all that she yearned for even though she could not see the vessel in the inky darkness: The clouds had again covered the moon, and the night was blacker than ever.

Tom had kicked off his shoes and retrieved a small lantern from beneath a pile of rocks where it had been hidden. Now he hunched over it, trying to light it. Antoine bent over him. The lamp flickered to life, and Tom scrambled up on a high rock. Antoine handed the lamp up to him, and the youth began signaling with it, a tiny pinpoint of light in a great black world.

They stared intently seaward, silently searching for some answering dot of light.

Nothing.

Antoine began to curse again. Diana prayed that no answer would come, that something had gone amiss and the smugglers' ship would fail them.

After a time, Tom gave up his signaling and jumped down from the rock. They waited fifteen minutes. Then Tom signaled again.

Blackness.

They waited another fifteen minutes. Then Tom signaled again.

This time, far across the water and so dim that they wondered at first whether it was their imagination, a faint prick of light answered them. It appeared and disappeared in a series of long and short flashes.

"They have put a boat in the water to fetch us," Tom said, interpreting the signals.

More minutes passed in silence, and Antoine began to pace nervously. Once he paused in front of Diana and, seeing her arms still tied, whipped out a dirk from a leather sheath that hung from his belt. As he did so, Diana saw he also had a pistol stuffed in his belt beneath his jacket. Cutting the ropes that bound her hands, he said, "The escape is now impossible."

But was it? she wondered as she shrank back against the rocks. The crashing waves cut off any escape on either side, but perhaps she might try to scramble back up the narrow, steep path that they had come down. But even as she contemplated that desperate move, she knew it was doomed to failure. Hampered as she was by her long petticoats, she would never be able to flee up the treacherous, rocky path fast enough to elude Antoine.

Antoine, who had begun pacing again, stopped suddenly and cocked his head. "The boat, do you not hear the oars?"

He was right. The slap of oars could be heard surprisingly near them by the left headland instead of straight out to sea.

"They musta gone wide of the mark," Tom said. "'Tis easy to do on a night black as this."

To Diana, the noise of the oars was like the sound of a mournful bell tolling her own doom. She could not bear it. She had to make one final effort, no matter how futile, to escape. Driven by her own anguish and despair, she picked up her petticoats, turned, and tried to flee up the path.

But Antoine saw her and hurled himself at her. They

crashed to the sand, she beneath him. She felt the cold, coarse dampness under her legs and realized to her horror that her skirts were tangled up about her thighs. Antoine forced her over on her back. She tried to push him away. But he only laughed and threw himself back down upon her. She squirmed beneath him, but the weight of his body had hers pinned securely to the ground.

He grabbed her hair and forced her head around so his mouth could fasten upon hers in a violent kiss.

Tom swung the lantern around and raised it so that they were framed in its light. "Hurry," he called in an urgent voice. "Plenty of time and then some you'll be having for lovemaking aboard the ship."

But Antoine did not heed him. Instead, he continued to hold her and force his punishing kiss upon her. The lamp played above them, illuminating their figures on the sand.

Diana thought of what would lie ahead of her that night and in the days before her aboard the smuggler's vessel. She was so overwhelmed by black despair that Tom's sudden violent cursing hardly registered upon her numb mind.

Then Antoine's weight was torn from her by violent hands.

CHAPTER 25

What happened next was a blur to Diana. She heard shouts and saw a man struggling with Tom on the sand. In all, four men had arrived in the boat. But Diana had eyes only for the one who had freed her from Antoine.

It was Alexander.

Diana's heart leaped with joy. "Oh, thank God," she murmured as she scrambled to her feet.

Alexander's fist crashed into Antoine's face, sending him staggering. He shook his head dazedly and backed away from Alexander, who went after him.

From the corner of her eye she saw Tom fall to the ground, knocked cold by the man with whom he had been fighting. Another man had snatched up the fallen lantern and held it high to illuminate the scene.

Suddenly, Antoine drew his pistol from his belt. "Now," he snarled at Alexander, "I shall have the pleasure of making your wife a very rich widow."

He raised the gun to put a ball through Alexander. With a lightning-quick movement, the duke drew his own pistol. Startled by the duke's speed, Antoine fired hastily, too hastily. Instead of striking Alexander in the heart as Antoine had intended, the ball sailed harmlessly through the left sleeve of his coat.

Alexander's shot followed a split second later and was far more accurate. Antoine crumpled to the ground, a red stain spreading slowly over his heart. Alexander dropped to his knee beside the man he had mortally wounded. A terrible rattle sounded in Antoine's throat; then his eyes froze, fixed and staring, in death.

Diana moved toward her husband. "Oh, Alexander, I was so afraid you would not come!"

He looked up at her, and she stopped dead in her tracks, frozen by the terrible look of excruciating pain, betrayal, rage, and disillusionment on his face. She needed no words to tell her that he had read the forged letter and had believed its contents.

And if that had not been enough, she realized with awful

clarity what the scene he had just witnessed on the beach must have looked like to him—his wife lying on the sand with Antoine atop her, the skirt of her gown gone, her petticoats about her thighs, her hair streaming out about her, locked in what appeared to be a passionate embrace and kiss with Antoine. Alexander must have heard, too, Tom's cry about plenty of time for lovemaking later.

Alexander rose slowly to his feet, the gun still in his hand, his face terrible to behold. He looked down at the gun he held. His voice, awful in its hollow emptiness, said, "It is fortunate for you, my faithless duchess, that there was not a second bullet in this gun or I should have put it through your black, treacherous heart."

With a final look of such revulsion that she was struck dumb, he turned from her and said to one of the three men who had accompanied him in the boat. "Take her away, Charlie."

For the first time, she realized that one of the trio who had been in the boat with Alexander was his brother. As Charlie stepped toward her, she eluded him and rushed after her husband, clutching desperately at the sleeve of his riding coat. "I love you, Alexander. You've got to believe me. Antoine abducted me by force. I swear he did."

Alexander jerked his arm away from her as though her touch disgusted him. "Don't think me an even greater fool than I already have been over you. If the letter you wrote me had not been enough to convince me of your perfidy, the scene I just witnessed left no doubt. So great was your passion for him you had not even the decency to wait for privacy but had to grovel in the sand with him." His words rang with contempt, and his face was filled with fury.

But deep in those gray eyes was such a look of unbearable agony that Diana instinctively reached out to comfort him.

He drew abruptly away from her touch, turned, and quickly walked across the sand. In a voice choked with misery, he said, "Charlie, for God's sake, take her away. Take her to Mistelay for me."

Obediently, Charlie, his face as grim as his brother's, took her arm and led her toward the small boat in which he and the others had landed.

The two men who had accompanied Alexander and Charlie stood back as Diana passed. She guessed that they were from the local constabulary. One was a middle-aged man with an authoritative bearing. The other was a younger man, who fell into step behind Diana and Charlie. When they were in the boat, he pushed it out into the tide and climbed in himself.

Alexander and the older man remained behind with Antoine's body and with Tom, who had been bound hand and foot and was lying like a trussed chicken against the rocks.

Once in the boat, Charlie and the other man plied the oars with vigor. Diana took off her kid slippers and poured the sand that had half filled them back into the sea.

The slap of the oars and the crash of the surf were the only sounds in the boat. No one spoke until, as they rowed around the headland, they passed another larger boat with more men headed toward the cove that they had just left.

"It is all over," the young man in Diana's boat called to the second vessel, "but there is a body and a prisoner for you to bring back."

A few minutes later he directed, "We pull in here."

As the boat bumped to a stop on the beach, Charlie scrambled out and helped Diana from it. A flight of rickety wooden stairs had been thrust into the side of the bluff to take them to the top.

Diana was so weak with fatigue and despair that she could hardly climb the shaky stairs. When at last she reached the top, a cabriolet was pulling to a stop beside a group of waiting horses, evidently belonging to the men who had gone in the boats. The cabriolet was guided by a youth of perhaps eighteen who stared at Diana and Charlie with frank curiosity. Once again, she was conscious of how wretchedly disheveled she looked.

Charlie quickly handed Diana into the cabriolet. He spent several minutes with the youth, apparently giving him directions, and then climbed in beside Diana. He radiated anger toward her, like a living reproach. She hoped that he would say something to break the awful silence, but he did not.

When she could bear it no longer, she asked softly, "How did you find us?"

"When your miserable letter was delivered, Alex guessed you and your lover would flee from where you had planned to go before." Charlie's usually mild voice was harsh and hating. "Our ride here from London was the fastest I have ever made in my life. The local authorities led us immediately to this stretch of coast, because it is the one most favored by smugglers. We rowed out offshore to watch for some sign or movement. Fortunately for us, your repeated signals with the lantern guided us directly to you."

"Charlie," Diana said in a breaking voice, "Antoine was not my lover. I hated him. I swear it. He abducted me and throttled me into unconsciousness when I tried to escape."

Her brother-in-law stiffened more rigidly on the seat beside her. "Just as he forced you to elope to the Red Fox Inn," Charlie burst out contemptuously. "Just as he forced you to kiss him this morning in your sitting room. Just as he forced you to write that evil letter to Alex. Just as Antoine was forcing you to lie with him on the beach just now when—"

"I was trying to flee, and he threw himself on me to stop me," she cried.

"Where were you trying to flee—up that path?"

She nodded.

"Of course you were," he snorted. "Only a mountain goat would have attempted that."

A weary, despairing sigh escaped from Diana's lips. "How can I make you believe that I love Alexander more than words can tell?"

"You cannot. Your treacherous actions speak far louder than your lying tongue."

"But why would I lie about it now?"

He turned blazing eyes upon her, eyes so like Alexander's when he was angry that she started. "Why, indeed? Now that your lover is dead and you have nowhere else to go. God, but Alex deserved so much better than you. That letter you wrote him this afternoon was the cruelest thing I have ever read. I will never forget his face as he read it." Charlie brushed his hand over his eyes. "You might as well have put a ball through his heart."

"The letter was a forgery. Antoine told me he paid a forger five pounds for it."

But Charlie seemed not even to hear her, so overcome was he by his anger. His fist crashed suddenly, violently, against the wood of the door. Diana jumped at such strong emotion from the usually placid Charlie.

"Damn you, Diana!" Charlie massaged his smarting fist. "Ah, the irony of it. How happy Alex was when he came back from Greycote. He told me, 'I think I would have offered for her even if she were penniless.'" Charlie stared blankly out the window. "I was so delighted that at last he had found a woman he cared for. What fools you made of us both."

Diana huddled miserably in a corner of the cabriolet, Charlie's words echoing and reechoing through her mind. If she could not convince Alexander's easygoing brother of her love and fidelity, how could she ever hope to convince Alexander himself? Her husband's face as he had stood on the beach over Antoine's body flashed before her, the agony and betrayal so deep and indelible in those gray eyes.

When at last they reached Mistelay, the first light of dawn

was coloring the eastern sky. Charlie instructed the youth to take the cabriolet around to a back entrance. "It's usually unlocked, and perhaps we can sneak in unnoticed." He tossed her his cloak. "In case we can't, wear this. It will at least conceal part of your bedraggled state."

Fortunately, the back door was open, and Diana was able to make her way up to her apartment unseen by anyone. Once safely inside it, she tossed Charlie's cloak aside. Lighting a candle, she walked with the candlestick over to a wall mirror, and she stared at her reflection. She hardly recognized herself. Her hair was a tumbled, tangled mess. Her face was smudged with dirt. The remains of her dress and her once-white petticoats were filthy and coated with sand. She looked, she thought, like a common slut after a hard night of plying her trade. Looking closer in the mirror, she saw the dark ugly bruises around her throat where Antoine had throttled her.

She would point them out to Charlie and to Alexander as proof of her veracity when she once again pleaded her case with them later in the day.

But when she awoke at noon, she found that Charlie had already departed for London. Alexander had not come at all.

All that day, which passed as slowly as eternity, Diana paced nervously through the vast, empty rooms of Mistelay, both longing for and dreading Alexander's arrival. But he did not come. Nor did he come the next day, or the next.

Instead, three days later a cart loaded with trunks and boxes containing all of her new wardrobe and other personal belongings arrived at Mistelay accompanied by a curt letter from Alexander that read:

Duchess:
    I have given instructions that you are to remain at Mistelay. Your father has decided that you will not attend his wedding, having so lately disgraced us all.

It would please me (therefore, I am certain that you will not do it) if you would devote yourself to restoring the house and gardens at Mistelay. All bills are to be forwarded to my secretary, Selwyn, for payment. You may hire what staff you need. You have my permission to bring whatever servants you wish from Greycote. However, I cannot permit Mrs. Cottam nor Tebbets to join you, since I trust them no more than I trust you.

Stratford

Diana folded the letter carefully, unable to hold back her tears. Even the good news that Tebbets was alive could not assuage her pain. The letter's salutation and the abrupt signature hurt her as much as the contents.

She wrote Alexander a long, impassioned letter, setting forth exactly what had happened and vowing her love for him. But the letter was returned unopened. A message from Selwyn attached to it read: "The duke wishes me to inform you that he will read no more letters from you. He said he has read one too many already and bade me return this to you unopened."

She sobbed as she finished the note. What was she to do? Alexander had forbidden her to come to London, so she could not plead her case to him personally, and he would not open her letters so that she could do so in writing. Her one slim hope was that as time passed, Alexander's anger and bitterness would recede and she would somehow be able to convince him of her love for him. It was this tiny glimmer, faint as it was, that kept her going.

But the weeks passed with no sign of Alexander or any word from him. Instead, Diana received a long letter from Mrs. Cottam, who was living with her sister, Mrs. Wise, in London. The epistle borrowed much from her sister's gossipy style:

My Dear Diana,

I did not want to write this letter, but my sister, Mrs. Wise, has been adamant in insisting that you would want to know and that it is my duty to inform you. The duke has been carrying on in the most outrageous manner with Lady Bradwell. They openly flaunt their liaison. I know that you predicted this would be how he would behave after your marriage, but I confess that I did not believe it of him. He seemed so considerate of you.

Meanwhile, the most dreadful stories, which I know are false, are circulating about you. I cannot image how they got started unless Lady Bradwell spread them to be-smirch your reputation.

The letter continued on at great length about the details of Landane's ostentatious wedding to Isabel and about the current London scandals, all of which, Diana gathered, were eclipsed by the one involving her, Alexander, and Lady Bradwell.

When Diana thought of that exquisite beauty with Alexander, she was consumed by agony. Unwittingly, thanks to Antoine, Alexander had been driven back to the waiting arms of Lady Bradwell. Antoine's revenge from the grave was complete, Diana thought bitterly.

She ran hastily upstairs to her apartment, where she threw herself across her bed and sobbed out her pain and grief. When her storm of tears had worn itself out, she turned over on her bed and stared up at the canopy. If only Alexander would come to Mistelay, since she was not permitted to leave. Surely, she told herself, he would come in May. He had told her how he loved it there in May.

But May came and passed slowly—oh, so slowly for Diana—without Alexander appearing. She wrote him letter after letter, but they all were returned unopened by Selwyn. From Alexander himself, she received no communication whatsoever.

Would he ever come to her again? Diana wondered in growing despair.

CHAPTER 26

On a fine day in June, with the elms and the chestnuts in full, luxurious leaf and the tiny white flowers of the privet and the yellow of the honeysuckle in rich bloom in the park, the duke of Stratford, in answer to an urgent summons from Mr. Stanley Pearce, presented himself at the latter's office in Fleet Street.

Pearce rose from behind his large desk, where even more papers were strewn about in even greater confusion than there had been on the duke's last visit. The barrister gestured toward a chair, and Alexander slumped into it. The old man's eyes, which matched his name, stared at Alexander from beneath the bushy brows in silence.

Although Mr. Pearce kept his wrinkled face impassive, he was startled by how worn and unhappy the duke looked on this visit. His dress, too, was uncharacteristically careless. His cravat was not arranged with its usual perfection, and his frock coat looked to have been donned in a slapdash fashion. His appearance did not measure up to the duke's normal impeccable standards. His gray eyes regarded the old man coldly.

As was his wont, Mr. Pearce wasted no time in preliminaries. "I should like to know, Your Grace, why you attempted to make me think worse of you than I need have when you sought my permission to marry Diana?"

Alexander straightened in surprise. "What are you talking about?"

"You were less than honest with me about your financial affairs."

"To the contrary, sir, everything I told you was quite true. I inherited a much-reduced fortune. My brother's gambling debts and my own extravagances added up to princely sums."

"Yes, all that was true enough, but you failed to tell me that by careful management of your estates and astute business dealings you considerably increased the fortune that you had inherited."

The duke's eyes glittered angrily. "I find your prying into my affairs both objectionable and inexcusable."

Pearce leaned back in his chair and tented his fingers together, resting the tips against his chin. "It seems that the duke of Stratford, who gave every appearance of being only an indolent, pleasure-loving rake with no thought to duty or business, managed both very quietly with most impressive results."

Alexander said coldly, "It would quite ruin my reputation if that were to get out. Furthermore, since you have so thoroughly investigated me, you must know that I am now in dreadful financial circumstances."

"Aye, but not because of your brother's gambling, your generosity to your lights of love, nor your management of your affairs." Mr. Pearce leaned farther back in his chair, but his eyes never left the younger man's face. "Instead, it was an incredible run of bad luck, a series of calamitous events over which you had no control: Napoleon's blockade of the continent, which cut off your business markets there; the great increase in taxes on everything from the number of servants to the number of windows—and you have huge numbers of both. Finally, the crop failure on your estates the past two years have left your many tenants not only unable to pay their rents to you but unable even to afford food. So you have spent vast sums that you no longer had to feed them, even selling off the furnishings at Mistelay to raise the money."

Pearce leaned forward suddenly, the front two legs of his chair coming down with a bang on the floor. "That, Your Grace, is why you are in dreadful financial situation. Even the king himself might have difficulty meeting that burden.''

Alexander shrugged, his face emotionless. "I cannot let my tenants starve. They are my responsibility."

"There are not many lords who feel as you do and even fewer who have taken it upon themselves to provide so well."

"You think me a fool?" Alexander asked coolly.

"No, I think you are exactly the man that both I and her grandfather would have wanted Diana to marry. But you would have saved me many qualms had you told me the truth. Why did you not?"

"I never dissuade people who wish to think the worst of me from doing so," he said coldly. "It costs me nothing, and it generally gives them great pleasure. I am curious, however, why you decided to investigate me now."

"Diana learned of your generosity to your tenants at Mistelay and wrote me of it. I was curious." Mr. Pearce gave a hoarse laugh that faded off into a thin cough. "I came to learn that I could not have found a more capable man in whose hands I could place her fortune."

"The duchess would not like that." It was the first time Alexander had mentioned his wife. His use of her title together with the bitter inflection with which he uttered it told Mr. Pearce that he still blamed her for much and forgave her for nothing.

Not that there was anything, in the old man's estimation, to forgive her despite the circumstances, which, even he had to admit, were overwhelmingly incriminating. "To the contrary, Your Grace. Diana has asked me to turn over control of her fortune—capital as well as income—to you."

Alexander's languor vanished, and the gray eyes studied Pearce's face intently. "Why should she do that?"

"She wishes to demonstrate her trust in you."

Alexander's gray eyes narrowed. "I wish I were able to reciprocate, but her faithlessness was too egregious."

Mr. Pearce slammed his aged hand, speckled with liver spots, down hard upon the desk in sudden anger. "If anyone has a right to complain of faithlessness, it is Diana of you, Your Grace. You are shockingly brazen about your scandalous affair with Lady Bradwell. Meanwhile, your poor wife is left alone and ignored at Mistelay. A gentleman would have suspended his affair with his mistress for at least a decent interval after he took a bride."

Alexander's gray eyes were flecked with anger. "I did not suspend my affair with Lady Bradwell. I ended it. And I had no intention of resuming it until my faithless wife sent me back, cuckolded and humiliated, to the willing lady's arms."

"Your wife was not faithless," Pearce shouted. "She was kidnapped by a scoundrel."

"I need only read the letter she sent me when she thought she had escaped me to know that is not true."

Pearce reached into the center drawer of his battered desk and drew out a document. "I have here proof that the letter to you was a forgery—more of Antoine's diabolic scheming." The old man handed the paper across the desk to Alexander. "It is a sworn statement by the forger that he was paid five pounds to produce it from letters Diana had sent to Antoine."

Alexander took the document, sworn to by one Oscar Poppin of Cheapside Lane, and glanced carelessly at it. Then he flipped it back across the desk to Pearce and asked in a soft, bored voice, "If for five pounds this Poppin will forge a false letter, what is his price for swearing to a false statement? Surely, Mr. Pearce, you cannot expect me to take this document seriously. Of course the duchess went willingly with Antoine, just as she was rolling in the sand with him when we reached them on the beach."

"She was trying to flee, and he fell on her to prevent her escape," Pearce insisted.

"What kind of chucklehead do you take me for?" Alexander snapped. "There was no way to escape that beach except by swimming."

"But Diana would have tried." Pearce again tented his fingertips, placing the tips against his nose, and studied Alexander quizzically.

"It puzzles me, Your Grace, why you would have forgiven Diana the transgression of trying to flee you before you were married—the only one of which she was guilty—when you are so adamant now in convicting her of something of which she is innocent. I myself was certain that night after she fled you that you would never marry her. Why did you?"

Alexander slumped in his chair and ran a weary hand, ornamented only with his black signet ring, through his equally black hair. "Because I believed myself to blame for her having fled. In my arrogance and my conceit—and I was guilty of those twin charges that she lodged against me—it never occurred to me that she would be anything but overjoyed to marry me. I made no attempt to court her. I did not even ask her to marry me; I told her I would. I thought she tried to flee to Antoine out of determination to escape me rather than any love for him." Alexander's eyes were filled with pain. "Subsequent events proved what a fool I was," he said bitterly.

"I swear to you, Your Grace, that Diana loves you and would not willingly do anything to hurt you." Pearce leaned over his desk, pleading with Alexander. "I shall gladly take an oath upon that."

"Ah, yes, she loves me so much she will not do the one and only thing I have asked of her. She will not restore Mistelay." The duke jumped up and began stalking up and down in front of Pearce's battered desk, much like a leashed dog on too short a rope. "You don't know how I long to be at Mistelay now. But when I think how dreadful it looks, the park a shambles, its lawns and gardens overgrown with weeds, the rooms as bare as a newly shorn sheep, I cannot bear to go there. It was the only thing I asked of her. But she has refused to do even that to accommodate me."

Alexander stopped his pacing and glared down at Mr. Pearce behind his battered desk. "And you try to tell me that she loves me."

"You don't know that she had done nothing. You have not been there to see it or her."

"I do not need to go. You don't know how eagerly I have scrutinized every bill, every account, that has come to me of her expenditures at Mistelay for some sign that she is making even the smallest effort to comply with my desires. But nothing!" Alexander resumed his agitated pacing. "Oh, it is true that she brought up the gardener from Greycote, but it would have taken thirty gardeners to even begin to chop away the ruin that is there now."

"She has made purchases for the house."

Alexander dismissed this declaration with an irritable toss of his head. "Some draperies, Chinese wallpaper, that sort of thing. But not one piece of furniture has she ordered, not one. Oh, yes, and she did hire a French chef." Sarcasm edged his voice. "She does seem to have an extraordinary fascination for all things French. She hires him when there is not even a table in the salon upon which to serve the meals he prepares."

"Your Grace, I beg of you. Go to Mistelay and see what Diana has or has not done. I am certain once she knows what you want, she will do whatever she can to please you."

"No," Alexander said flatly. "I shall give her no more opportunities to humiliate and mock me."

"But you cannot go on like this with your wife at Mistelay and you here in London."

"No, and it is not my intention to do so. When the worst of the scandal has died down, I shall endeavor to divorce her quietly." Alexander stalked from the room before Mr. Pearce could say another word.

CHAPTER 27

Diana stood restlessly at a window in the ducal apartments at Mistelay and looked out over the gardens. The mail was late that day. If only a letter would come from Mr. Pearce. It had been a whole week since he had met with Alexander to plead her case. The old man had promised that he would notify her immediately of the meeting's outcome. But as the days had passed with no word from him, Diana knew the reason for his silence. Alexander had not been persuaded. Still, she longed to hear some word, any word, of her husband.

The window at which she stood commanded a fine view of the gardens, and she could not help but be pleased at the fruits of her labor, so evident below her. Gone was the overgrown tangle that had been there when first she had arrived. Beneath the window the yew hedges that formed the parterres of the Elizabethan garden had been clipped back and tamed to reveal the garden's intricate geometric pattern. The flower beds within the encircling yew, once barren, were masses of color, one to each bed and carefully harmonized with its neighbors so that now the garden looked like a brightly patterned carpet of blue, white, yellow, pink, and lilac.

Beyond the garden the carefully weeded lawn, a rolling field of lush green, marched to the edge of the park. The serpentine lake had been cleaned of its scum, and water lilies once again floated serenely on its surface, their white blooms and green pads a handsome contrast against the placid water.

The undergrowth that had choked the park had been hacked away, and once again it provided an idyllic setting for a pleasant walk. The great elm, chestnut, and oak trees had been pruned and shaped.

How proud she was of what she had created out of neglect and chaos. Inside and out, Mistelay was once again a place of beauty. Perhaps because she had been forced to make such stringent economies during her years at Greycote, she took pride, too, in how little it had cost her to transform Mistelay. The years of careful management that had been forced upon her at Greycote were not easily forgotten and continued to guide her even now.

Diana turned from the window, well pleased with the scene below her. How surprised Alexander would be to see the transformation she had wrought. If only he, for whom it was all meant, would come to see it. Diana sighed and looked anxiously at the gilt bronze clock on a red marble plinth. She was relieved to see that she had at least another hour of peace before the well-meaning Mrs. Gill would seek her out, as she sought her out each day, to try to persuade Diana to eat a luncheon for which she had no appetite.

As the weeks had passed with no word from Alexander, her interest in food had shrunk along with her waist until now the wardrobe that he had ordered hung loosely on her. Diana did force herself to eat small amounts to mollify Louis, the temperamental French chef she had hired at an outrageous wage to tempt Alexander's palate when he came to Mistelay. But as the weeks passed, it looked less likely that he would ever sample Louis's superb fare, and Diana was thinking of letting the chef go. Such a waste to keep him, she thought as she left the apartment and headed downstairs.

The mail had just come, and she reached hastily for the letter. To her enormous relief she saw it was from Mr. Pearce.

Quickly, she opened it. As she read, the eagerness disappeared from her face and was replaced by grief. The letter was short, for Mr. Pearce wasted no words when he wrote. It told her bluntly of Alexander's bitter response to her wish to turn her fortune over to him, of his flat refusal to go to see her at Mistelay, and of his plan to divorce her eventually.

"Nothing can persuade the duke that you were abducted by Antoine. I fear the scene he witnessed when he found you on the beach has closed his heart to you forever," Pearce wrote.

Diana's shoulders sagged in despair as she folded the letter and contemplated the bleakness of her future. Divorce. So it had come to that. Tears spilled from her eyes at the realization that Alexander would never again hold her in his arms.

She felt crushed by despair. With dragging feet, she went into the music room overlooking the side terrace and sat down at her harp, pouring out her sorrow in a song of wrenching sadness. The melancholy chords fell like tears from her harp. Her voice joined the harp. It, too, was colored with sorrow.

As she sang, Diana was beset by the uneasy feeling that she was not alone. Glancing around, she saw Alexander slumped behind her in a brocade Louis XV armchair, his face a strange mask. There was a disconcerting remoteness in the depths of his gray eyes, as though he were watching her from another world.

"Alexander," she gasped, "I did not hear you come." In her shock, her suddenly nerveless fingers slid across the strings of the harp in a sharp squawk of dissonance. Recovering herself, she got up from the harp and said, her voice trembling with nervousness, "What a happy surprise."

He rose as she did and came toward her. "Is it?" he asked in a voice as hollow and emotionless as his face. How weary he looked, she thought. His black hair was tousled. The day was hot, and he had unbuttoned his brown riding coat. His white shirt of finest linen was tucked into buckskin breeches that fitted perfectly his slim hips. The customary high polish of his black Wellington boots had been veiled by a thick layer of gray dust that signified he must have come on horseback.

"Why did you come down on horseback?" she asked.

"I intended only a very brief stop."

She choked on her disappointment. "Surely you will at least stay for dinner. I am most anxious to have your opinion of the French chef I have hired."

"Why do you want my opinion when your own of him is so poor?"

"But no," she stammered in confusion, "I find him excellent. Why would you think I did not?"

He gave her a critical perusal, and his eyes had a strange look in them that she could not decipher. "From the look of you, it appears that you have given up eating altogether. You are so very thin."

She forced lightness into her voice. "Better too thin than too fat."

"I count neither desirable."

They stood awkwardly facing each other. Diana's heart thumped wildly as she tried to read in Alexander's impenetrable gray eyes his emotions toward her.

"I see that Mistelay is much changed since last I was here," he said at last.

"Let me show you it," she cried eagerly. "I so hope that you will like what I have done."

She began the tour with the state rooms. They had been redone in all the formality demanded by their ornate vastness, with the high moulded ceilings garlanded and muraled.

Alexander said nothing as she led him through room after room. She watched his face anxiously as he studied her handiwork, but he gave not the slightest clue to his thoughts.

Everywhere one looked there were priceless pieces of French furniture wrought by the most renowned craftsmen from the finest woods and decorated with marquetry inlays in intricate patterns, ormolu mounts, and Sevres porcelain plaques. The rooms very nearly rivaled Versailles in the splendor of their furnishings, which had been arranged with an eye that robbed them of the uncomfortable stiffness usually found in such chambers. Mistelay's great art collection had been restored to its proper place of honor on the walls, brightened with moiré coverings and newly painted wainscoting.

In contrast to the state apartments, the other downstairs rooms had been done more informally, with French provincial furniture and an eye for comfort and color. Upholstery and draperies were in bright floral patterns.

Still Alexander did not speak, and by now Diana was far too nervous to talk, either. The cold gray eyes had missed nothing, but neither had they softened. If anything was to be read in them as the tour progressed, it was a look of deep and growing irritation. Diana's heart sank. She had tried so hard to redo Mistelay in the way she had thought he would most like, but instead he obviously hated it.

They made their way, still in silence, up the broad staircase to the upstairs. The door of the nursery was half-open. Alexander stopped and stared in. It seemed to be two very different rooms. On one half, Diana had painted the walls with characters from nursery rhymes: plump blackbirds flapping up from a startled king's pie; cherub-faced Jack and Jill tumbling, bucket in hand, down the hill; a fat, egg-shaped Humpty-Dumpty sitting on his wall. Then the characters stopped abruptly, as if the artist had suddenly died midway through the work.

Alexander's critical demeanor deepened into a frown as he regarded the room. Diana cringed with embarrassment. Her sophisticated husband must be appalled that she had painted silly pictures on the walls for children that, given his hatred of her, would never be born.

"Why did you stop so abruptly with it half-done?" It was the first time Alexander had spoken to her since they had begun their tour of the house.

She colored. "I thought . . . I hoped I might . . . but . . . but I wasn't," she replied incoherently.

His right eyebrow arched questioningly. "Were you disappointed?" His calm tone held no clue to his emotions.

"At first I was, but then I was glad. It was for the best."

"Why? Do you not think I would be a good father?"

She stared miserably down at the floor. "An excellent one if you believed that you were."

"Was there any reason for me to doubt it?" His voice was brittle.

"No, none," she said firmly, her eyes meeting his unhesitatingly, "but I was afraid that you would."

He said nothing, only watched her with those inscrutable gray eyes until she burst out, "I could not bear for an innocent child to suffer for—for—" She broke off, too choked by emotion to continue.

"For the sins of his mother?" Alexander concluded for her.

Her eyes heated with anger. "There was no sin, I swear to you!"

His face was set in grim lines. "That was most difficult to believe after that scene I witnessed on the beach."

"If only you would believe the truth of what happened," she cried in anguish. "I was trying to escape him. I knew it was hopeless, but I had to try. If only you knew how loathsome Antoine was to me." She was no longer able to hold back her tears. She turned and fled from the room.

As she ran down the hall, she heard Alexander behind her. Blindly, she opened the first door she came to and hurried inside, trying to slam the door after her.

But he caught it and followed her in. She heard him gasp in surprise. Wiping at her eyes, blinded by her tears, she saw that they were in the ducal bedchamber.

She turned to face him but found that he had forgotten Antoine, her, and seemingly everything else as he stared in wonder at the change that had been wrought in his bedchamber.

The threadbare, faded gray velvet was gone from the walls, the windows, and the bed. It had been replaced by silk hangings of pale yellow. The massive carved bed had given way to one with delicate fluted posts. Louis XV chairs covered in yellow brocade were scattered about. A carved mahogany reading table, its top pushed up as though in readiness for its master, stood by one of the windows. The room was now as cheerful and inviting as it previously had been dark and dismal.

Alexander stopped by a small mahogany cupboard and rubbed his finger absently on the marble top. Suddenly, he turned angrily to Diana. "Why the blazes didn't you let me know what you were doing here with the house and the grounds?"

Her heart seemed to shrivel within her. All her work had been in vain. Alexander hated it. "I tried," she stammered. "I wrote you letter after letter telling you what I was doing and asking your advice, but they were all returned to me unopened by Selwyn."

Diana's shoulders sagged with despair. Never in her life had she felt so utterly defeated and hopeless. "I thought this was what you wanted. I am sorry you don't like it." Unable to bear the strange, irritated look in his gray eyes, she rushed on. "We can change what you don't like. I am sorry I have not done it the way you wanted it. I tried to. Oh, Alexander, I meant only to please you, but instead I have made a mull of it." A choked sob escaped from her throat.

In two quick strides, Alexander was before her. He wrapped her in his arms and held her to him. "Believe me, my darling Diana, it is all beautiful. I could not be more delighted with everything that you have done."

"Why did you look so strange, then?" she asked, unable to believe that she was in his arms again.

"When I saw how beautiful it all was, I was so unhappy that I had not come before. I would have had I known what you were about. Instead, I have been furious because I thought you were deliberately ignoring my request to restore Mistelay, which I took as one more sign that in your heart you cared naught for me."

"But why did you think I was doing nothing?" Diana asked in bewilderment.

"There were no bills. I still cannot understand how you managed somehow to assemble a priceless collection of furniture without apparently spending a sixpence. I know that you are famous for your skill as a household manager, but this goes beyond credulity." He held her out slightly from him and said with a teasing smile, "Tell me. Do you have a fairy godmother who, at your command, waves her magic wand and *voilá!* Furniture appears?"

Diana giggled, her heart soaring. "Only a fairy grandfather who left me his collection of furniture from his house in Mayfair. It has been in storage since his death."

"So I behold the famous Wakely collection. But how did you ever manage to reclaim the grounds from the jungle without hiring an army of gardeners?"

She smiled shyly at him, her arms creeping around him. "I have you to thank for that. Your tenants were so grateful for all that you have done for them the past months that they asked me what they could do to repay you. I put them to work on the grounds. With all those hands, it went very quickly."

His gray eyes, gleaming with amused appreciation, stared down at her. She still could not believe the change in him. A shadow fell over her heart as she remembered what he had said about making only a brief stop at Mistelay. If he were to leave now, she could not bear it. Throwing her dignity to the wind, she pleaded, "Please, Alexander, please, I beg of you to let me return to London with you."

His face turned grave. "I am afraid, Diana, it may be many months before I can permit you to go back there."

"Why?" she cried in despair. "Are you still determined to punish me for something I did not do? Why won't you believe the truth? I hated Antoine! Oh, Alexander, why won't you believe me?"

"I do believe you."

He spoke so quietly that it was a moment before Diana fully comprehended what he had said. Her arms dropped limply away from him, and fear laced her voice. "Then why won't you permit me to return to London?"

He took her gently in his arms again. "Because I want you to stay here with me." He smiled down at her with such tenderness in his gray eyes that she wanted to weep with joy. "Now that I have seen what you have created here, London may never see my face again. I prefer spending my days here, enjoying Mistelay beside the woman I love."

He wrapped her in a fierce embrace and kissed her with a

passion that left her no doubt about the veracity of his words.

It was some time before he released her, and by then she was both breathless and glowing with rapture.

"Oh, Alexander, to have you hold me like that. It is all that I have dreamed of these endless lonely weeks."

"It must have been very lonely by yourself here," he said softly, his arm still about her.

"That was not the reason. I would have been lonely anywhere you were not."

He nodded. "I know how lonely I am where you are not." He reached into his coat. "By the way, I have some property of yours to return to you." He drew out two folded letters and handed them to her.

Puzzled, she opened them and found the first was the letter she had written Antoine from Greycote. The second was the brief note, which she had penned in London, telling Antoine that she hated him and never wanted to see him again.

"Where did you get these?" she asked.

"I bought them back from the forger who wrote that wretched letter for Antoine. The man's address was on the sworn statement that Mr. Pearce showed me last week, and I decided I would pay Mr. Poppin a visit. I wanted so much, my darling Diana, to believe your story, but it was so difficult for me after that forged letter and the scene on the beach. How relieved I was to see this other note to Antoine that verified what you had been saying."

Alexander's gray eyes twinkled with amusement. "It was a most edifying visit. Poppin lived just off the alley where you were switched from my carriage into another coach. While I was there, I chanced to meet a woman upon whom you made a lively impression with the fight that you gave Antoine and his accomplice."

Diana remembered the thin woman and the ragged children that she had seen at the alley mouth.

Alexander smiled and stroked his wife's face tenderly. "I was both proud and delighted to learn that your spirit and courage did not desert you under even the most terrifying circumstances, my little spitfire. Any other female of my acquaintance would have been in strong hysterics, if she had not already fainted dead away."

"I hardly see that *those* tactics would have aided my escape," she remarked dryly.

"The woman told me how Antoine had to throttle you into submission." His fingertips gently touched her throat as if to reassure himself that it was now undamaged. "Charlie had noticed the bruises about your neck when he took you to Mistelay, but it was not until I talked to her that I realized their significance. If I had not already killed Antoine, I would have then." He clasped Diana to him again, murmuring, "My own dear love."

"Do you truly love me?" she asked, staring up at him with questioning eyes.

He hugged her tightly to him again. "Ninnyhammer. I know you think I made you an offer only for your money, but you were dead wrong."

She grinned back. "I suppose it was my beautiful yellow skin and dingy hair?"

Alexander laughed. "You know, I saw through your silly disguise quite quickly. And thanks to the storm that kept me at Greycote, I discovered you were as different a woman within as you were without. Seeing you with the Hill children told me you would make an excellent mother. You ran an exemplary household, but most important, you had a lively intelligence and a sense of humor—even if I was the butt of it that first night. By the time I made my offer, I considered myself lucky to have found such a gem."

"That is not the way you either looked or sounded when you told me you would marry me," she told him tartly.

"I made a terrible mull of that, didn't I? The truth was

that for the first time in my life I was at a loss as to how to fix a woman's interest. You were so different from anyone I had yet known, and you had told me you were not in the least romantic. For the first time in my life my heart was engaged in my suit. So all my polished address quite deserted me, and I blundered ahead disastrously.''

Diana's eyes sparkled dangerously. "You hadn't the slightest doubt, my lord duke, that I would accept your offer.''

"That's true," he admitted. "I thought my proposal, if I were not careful, might become the butt of one of your wickedly funny imitations to our children and grandchildren, but it never occurred to me that you would find the offer truly offensive. I was stunned and infuriated to learn that you actually thought I was proposing merely to secure your fortune.''

"You did not deny it," she reminded him.

"You misunderstood. What I did not deny was that your money was one of the considerations that drew me to Greycote.''

"What other considerations could there possibly have been?''

"You sounded like a woman of spirit and humor to me, and I was right." He hugged her to him again.

"If I was such a gem, why did it take you so long after we were wed for you to even bother to consummate our marriage? Were you still angry about my trying to run away?''

"You silly goose, I was courting you. You were quick to point out to me that night at the Red Fox Inn that I had not bothered to do so. Under the circumstances, I had no time to rectify the situation before we were married, so I tried to do so afterward. I wanted you to come willingly to me.''

His hands caressed her intimately, bringing back memories of that night. She smiled with pleasure. "It was a beautiful night," she murmured.

"Then why were you so cold and resistant the next night?" he asked, still caressing her.

Even now, in the comforting shelter of Alexander's arms, Diana stiffened as she remembered Lady Bradwell sitting triumphantly in her box with the emeralds Alexander had given her glittering at her neck.

Diana drew back from her husband. "What about Lady Bradwell?"

He bent his head and kissed Diana's lips slowly and tenderly. "My darling Diana, you have two things of mine that Lady Bradwell nor, for that matter, any other woman has ever had—my name and my love."

Diana recalled what her brother-in-law had said about the necklace. "Charlie said the emeralds you gave Lady Bradwell were your farewell present to her. Is that true?"

"Yes." Sudden understanding shone in Alexander's gray eyes. "So that was what was bothering you that night of the theater. Here I thought it was Antoine, and it was only that blasted necklace."

"Not the necklace. I thought you must have been with her that day to have known she would be at the theater."

"Good God, Diana, I had not seen her since I had given her that necklace. I swear to you."

"I believe you," she said softly. "But she is an exquisite creature." Diana's face grew mischievous. "And so is her necklace."

His eyes gleamed teasingly. "I have told you before, my love, emeralds do not suit you."

"They don't?" Diana's blue eyes flashed dangerously.

"Definitely not. Sapphires and diamonds are your stones. Sapphires to match your eyes and diamonds to match your brilliance."

She giggled happily at his nonsense. Suddenly, he smothered her in another urgent embrace, pressing her to him so tightly that she could scarcely breathe. His lips closed over hers in a long, demanding kiss. Never had Diana thought it was possible to be so happy as she was at that moment.

When finally he lifted his lips from hers, she looked up at him with an irrepressible gleam in her eyes. "And is it true—does Lady Bradwell bore you, my lord duke?"

"Definitely, my lady duchess. As much, in fact, as you delight me," he assured her, kissing her again.